A dark, dense, subtle portrait of the intricate continuum of urban life—and death—done in such bold strokes and shapes that you will never see the city the same way again.

— Kirkpatrick Sale
author of *Rebels Against the Future*

His trademark woodcut effect owes a debt to the European tradition of picture-book social commentary...a continuous narrative that pans like a Steadicam.

— Sam Pratt
SPIN

Kuper's brilliant visual novel, much like Fritz Lang, creates comic noir of corruption and innocence in a city where the devil is always in the details.

— Sue Coe
author of *Sheep of Fools*

His storytelling is as daring and fluid as a teenage skateboarder's movements, braiding the many threads of the story together with jaw-dropping panache.... An absolute *tour de force*.

— Douglas Wolk
CMJ

In his wordless graphic novel, THE SYSTEM, Peter Kuper captures the energy of New York City in the '80s and '90s. Class and caste are portrayed in stark pantomime. Archetypal characters race, hustle, push, and shove their way down the corridors of a serpentine plot in a city where everyone is connected but nobody notices it. Following in the foot-steps of Charlie Chaplin, Kuper shows us a precarious world constantly on the edge of destruction that somehow saves itself, if only to fall into chaos again in the next panel. Yeah, that's our New York City!

— Seth Tobocman
author of *War in the Neighborhood*

THE SYSTEM is truly a visual feast.
— Kent Worcester
The Comics Journal

THE SYSTEM paints a complex portrait of a place in which many stories are unfolding, intersecting, and symbolically feeding off one another. That locus is the mega-metropolis of New York City, where the poorest of the poor and the richest of the rich act out the ironies of postmodern civilization on a daily basis.
— Matt Ashare
Boston Phoenix

Peter Kuper's beautiful drawings take you on a tour of the secret places in a dark and ominously silent universe you will never forget.
— Gahan Wilson
cartoonist, the *New Yorker*

Never pass up a new Kuper title. His talent for telling a story is too good to ignore, and his blunt stencil art is just as wonderful.
— Mark Frauenfelder
Wired

Peter Kuper's THE SYSTEM is pushing the perimeters of this medium—Bravo!
— Will Eisner
creator of *The Spirit*

Peter Kuper's THE SYSTEM is just like New York—totally sleazy and totally cool.
— Bill Plympton
animator of *Guard Dog*

THE
SYSTEM

By

Peter Kuper

Introduction by Calvin Reid

First edition, April 2014
ISBN: 978-1-60486-811-1
Library of Congress
Control Number:
2013956916
Printed in Singapore

Published by
PM Press
PO Box 23912
Oakland, CA 94623
510-658-3906
info@pmpress.org

ABOUT PM PRESS
PM Press was founded at the end of 2007 by a small collection of folks
with decades of publishing, media, and organizing experience. PM Press
co-conspirators have published and distributed hundreds of books,
pamphlets, CDs, and DVDs. Members of PM have founded enduring book fairs,
spearheaded victorious tenant organizing campaigns, and worked closely with
bookstores, academic conferences, and even rock bands to deliver political
and challenging ideas to all walks of life. We're old enough to know what we're
doing and young enough to know what's at stake.
For more information please visit us at www.pmpress.org

Also by the author
from PM Press

Diario de Oaxaca

Drawn to New York

World War 3 Illustrated 1979–2014
(coedited with Seth Tobocman)

Dedicated to
Lou Stathis

PREFACE

When editor Lou Stathis first approached me in 1995 about creating something for DC Comics, I wondered what I might produce that could find a home in a world of fantasy. Up to that point my comics had illustrated painfully real (and embarrassing) autobiographical and political subjects, and appeared in alternative, underground publications. Lou explained that DC's new Vertigo Vérité imprint was aiming for an audience beyond comic shops. It had been my hope and crusade for decades to get graphic novels into the hands of non-traditional comic book readers, though I didn't imagine there was a chance of achieving that through Superman's publisher.

Yet, Lou's request was the nudge I needed to excavate a story idea that had been building up in my file drawers for about eight years. The concept was sparked as I raced to the New York Times for an illustration assignment. Same train line, same last car, but this time as my eyes passed over my fellow passengers I started wondering about their destinations. Was this trip all we had in common, or might our lives crisscross and impact one another in positive or even catastrophic ways? If the flap of a butterfly's wings in China could cause a storm in Manhattan, what would the various actions of a subway full of commuters incite?

I proposed THE SYSTEM as a picture story without text. Wordless comics eliminate language barriers and invite readers to interpret the visuals and invent dialogue. This also removed a comic book convention: the word balloon, a visual cue that led non–comic book readers to dismiss the form as one indistinguishable genre. To further confound expectations (and my chances of getting it published), I took the ridiculously labor-intensive approach of stencil cutting and spray painting each page and allowing panels to bleed into one another. I anticipated Superman would reject my whole approach, but he (and other un-costumed individuals) embraced it, and THE SYSTEM appeared in three consecutive monthly comic books followed by a collected paperback edition.

In the nearly twenty years since I produced THE SYSTEM, graphic novels have gone through a renaissance. They have become part of the literary canon and are featured prominently in libraries, galleries, and museums. Hell, I've even found myself teaching a course on comics at Harvard, something unthinkable when THE SYSTEM was first published.

Though I still live in New York City, where this story is set, most of the locales I referenced have been obliterated. Times Square has morphed into Disneyland, Checker cabs are history, and cell phones have gotten smaller while insider-trading scandals have grown to monstrous proportions. Gone are the iconic Twin Towers, blown to dust along with thousands of lives. Also gone is my editor Lou Stathis, taken by cancer mere months after the book's original publication. All a reminder of how fragile the system actually is.

—Peter Kuper
New York City, 2014

BRIGHT LIGHTS,

When Peter Kuper draws, people take notice. I certainly did the first time I encountered *New York, New York,* Kuper's first collection of comics. That book provided a glimpse of Kuper's knack for combining witty social vignettes with a striking, eye-grabbing graphic and for adding an equally insistent layer of autobiographical insight to a series of sharply drawn, gritty, sometimes surreal urban scenarios. These early comics captured an incipient ability to wring an instructive and comic sensibility out of the everyday, existential calamity of life in New York.

All this is to say that Peter Kuper has taken his place among a group of thoughtful, creatively neurotic comics artists instrumental to the latest transformation of American comics. If the countercultural underground comics of the 1960s released American comics from both the suppressive effects of the Comics Code Authority and the commercial domination of a new generation of superheroes (and they did), then this group of neo-undergrounders has managed to build on that legacy in the 1980s and 1990s, expanding on the kinds of comics produced by people like Robert and Aline Kominsky Crumb, Justin Green, Diane Noomin, Art Spiegelman, and so many others from that funkily seminal period.

You have to go back to *MAD* magazine in the 1950s or the styish newspaper strips of the 1920s and 1930s to find such a refreshing and innovative period in American comics as we find ourselves today. Indeed, the best of today's "alternative comics" seem to have borrowed the best of that 1960s generation—the hilariously outrageous mix of political and social satire, drug humor, sexual self-revelation, and vivid, eclectic graphic styles—adding their own contemporary varieties of social compulsions, familially inflicted neurosis, and political outrage to the creative mix to give this generation of artists its own stamp, cast, and sensibility.

So it was not surprising that his work and interests developed into the graphically eclectic, relentless social criticism of *World War 3 Illustrated,* the well-known semiannual anthology of political comics that he cofounded and coedits; or delightfully observant first-person travel accounts collected in *ComicsTrips.* But it's in his hilariously revealing "Unauthorized Autobiography," *Stripped,* and in *Give It Up!,* a graphic meditation on Kafka's dark literary conundrums, that we're treated to the full impact of his talent for narrative invention, social depiction, inspired comedy, and, in *Give It Up!,* a sympathetic, vividly imagined literary collaboration—coaxing his comics into the sublime realm of symbol, myth, and the deeper mysteries of human consciousness.

Since this essay was first published in the late 1990s, Kuper's managed to broaden his work into an ever-expanding range of formats and newly discovered urban neuroses. In 2007, he expanded and reformulated his earlier autobiographical work in *Stop Forgetting to*

Remember, a bio-graphic (in every sense of the word) post-9/11, postpartum recap of the life of Walter Kurtz—his undisguised alter ego—a typically desperate cartoonist, now turned doting parent, facing newly intensive levels and forms of vividly delineated, reliably hilarious, urban existential dread. He also revisited Franz Kafka in 2003 with a typically personal, expressionistic reinterpretation of *The Metamorphosis*, which has since been adopted by high school and university curriculums around the United States and has been translated into nine languages.

There's much more—producing work, whether iconic illustrations or funny, thoughtful comics, never seems to be much of a problem for him. From taking over *Spy vs. Spy, MAD* magazine's wordless, pricelessly dopey espionage comic, to the extraordinary *Diario de Oaxaca: A Sketchbook Journal of Two Years in Mexico*, a copious and richly inventive collection of sketches, comics, portraits and still lifes, to *Drawn to New York*, a similar display of Kuper's graphic chops tracing, documenting, and recapitulating a lifetime of loving and drawing New York City.

Originally published in 1997, THE SYSTEM serves as an early repository of all his influences, graphic achievements, and attempts to reconcile comics to their own formal history, to life and to art, and specifically to the knockabout experience of life in New York City. His use of stencils, the ordinary graphic tool of sign painters and political activists, has developed into a dynamic and wholly original illustrative style as energetic and as insistently entertaining as life in Gotham, a cityscape often vividly decorated with stencil art.

A wordless pictorial novel reminiscent of Frans Masereel's *Passionate Journey*, THE SYSTEM is a parable-like, sentimental meditation on the convulsive social drama of day-to-day urban life. It weaves its multiple narrative threads into a brightly patterned fabric of recognizable, fictionalized events—a kind of melodrama on the patterns of city life. Kuper's notion of the urban "system" is an elaborate network of coincidental encounters, parallel routines and, most important, the overlapping, interdependent tales of disparate social and politicized interests that loom over the lives of ordinary people, from strippers and crooked cops to martyred street artists, corporate financiers, and Pakistani cab drivers.

THE SYSTEM details the capricious power of coincidence, the simple bonds of affection, the daily grind, and the super-charged existential consequences of ethnic and social complexity—and illuminates it all with the glow of New York City's scary magnificence.

—Calvin Reid
New York City, 2014

Calvin Reid is a senior news editor at *Publishers Weekly* and coeditor of *PW Comics World, PW*'s online and print comics news journal.

"I must
create a
system or
be enslaved by
another man's."

—WILLIAM BLAKE

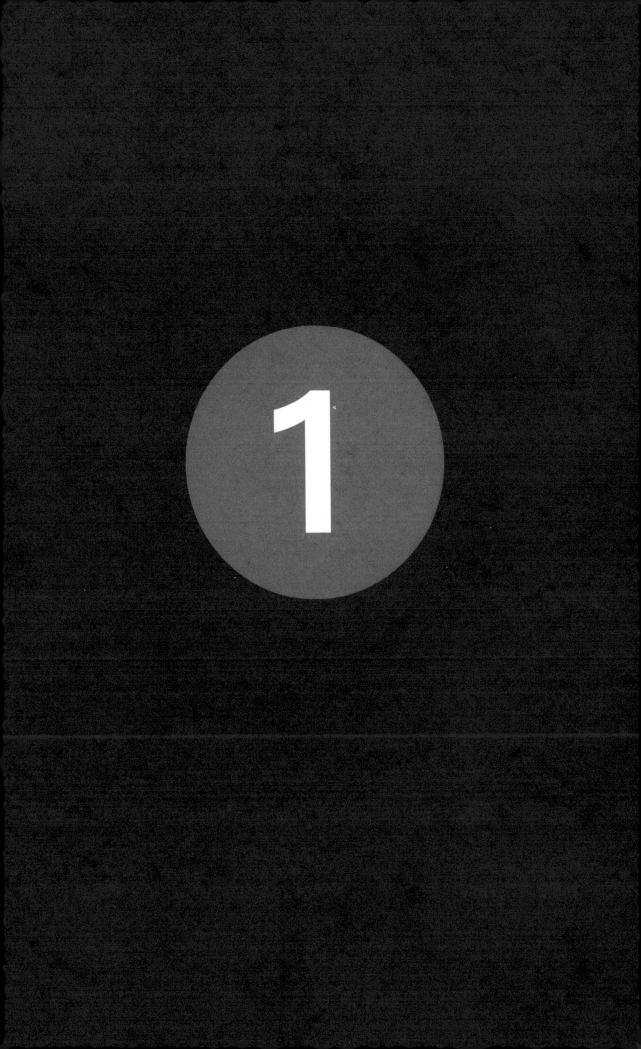

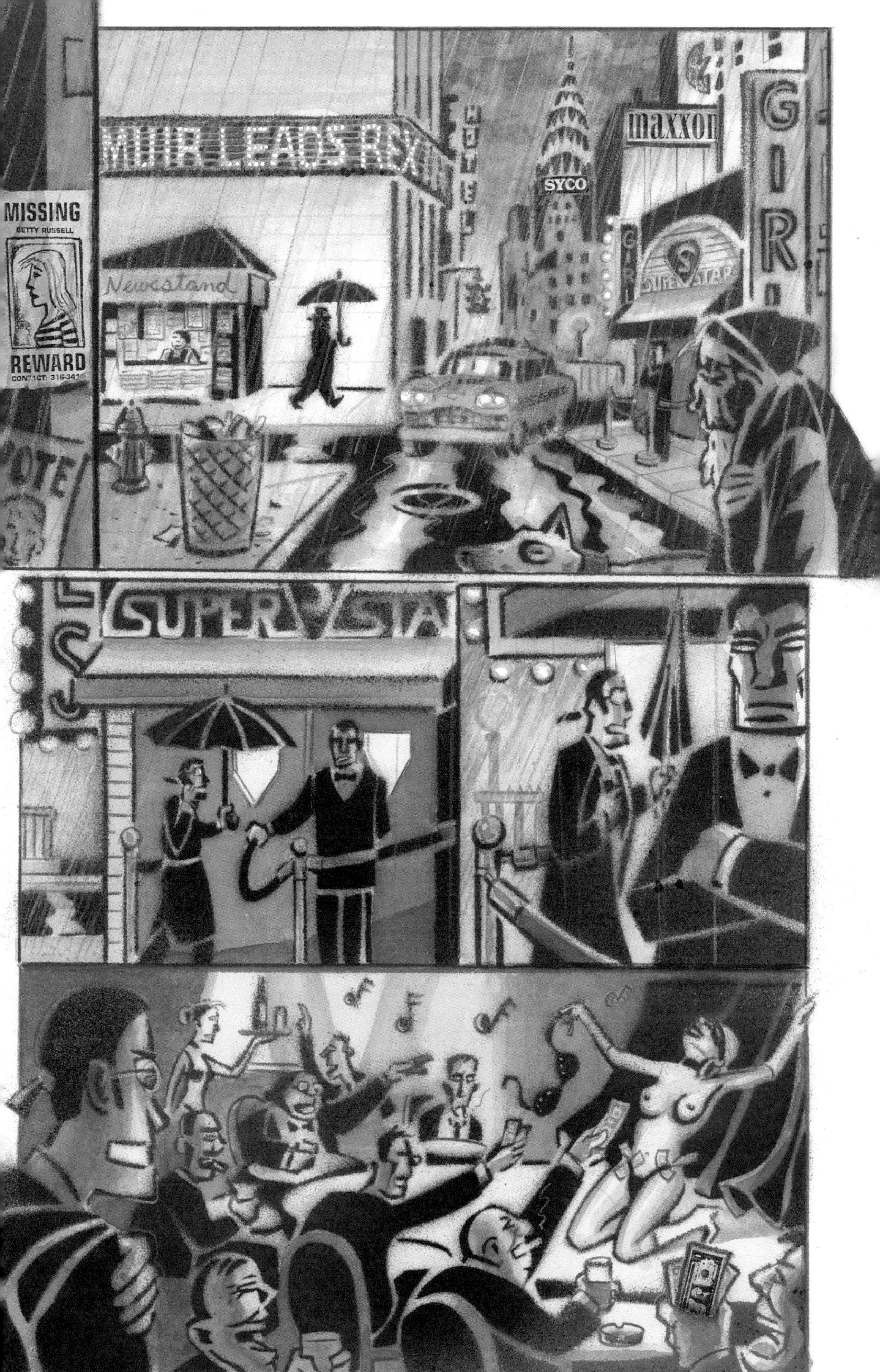
MISSING
BETTY RUSSELL
REWARD
Newsstand
HOTEL
SYCO
maxxon
SUPERSTAR

EXIT

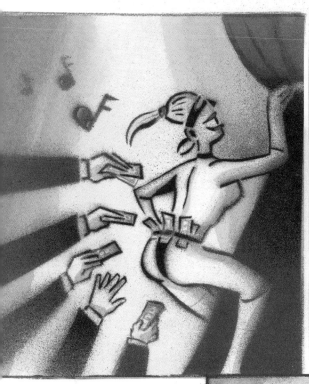

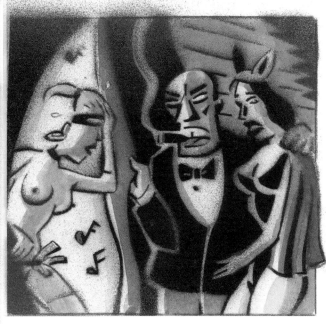

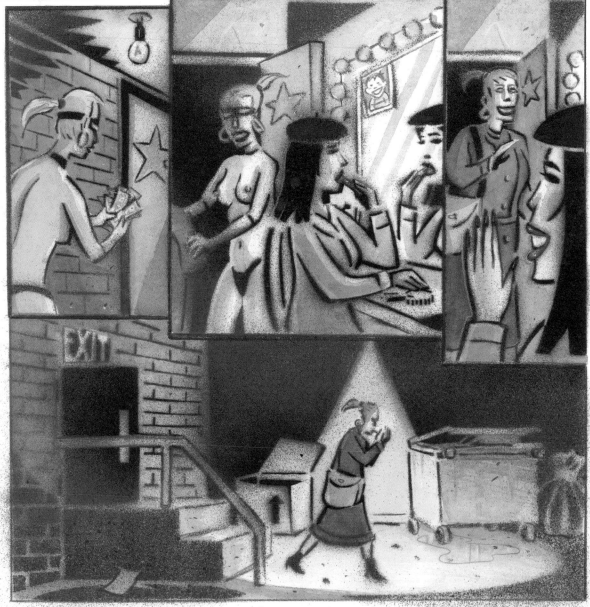

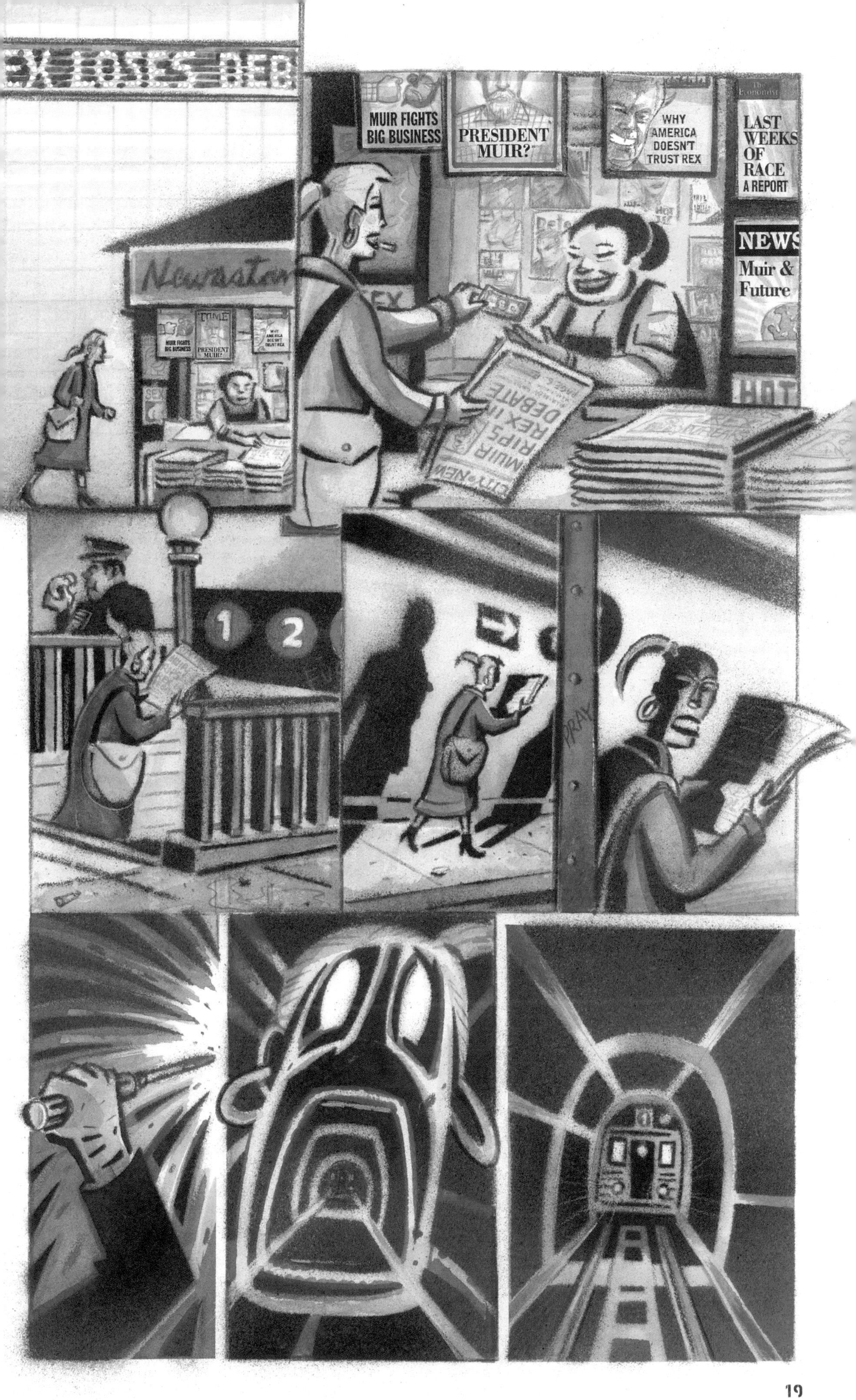

MUIR FIGHTS BIG BUSINESS
PRESIDENT MUIR?
WHY AMERICA DOESN'T TRUST REX
LAST WEEKS OF RACE A REPORT
NEWS Muir & Future
Newsstand
MUIR RIPS REX IN DEBATE
CITY NEWS
1
2
PRAY

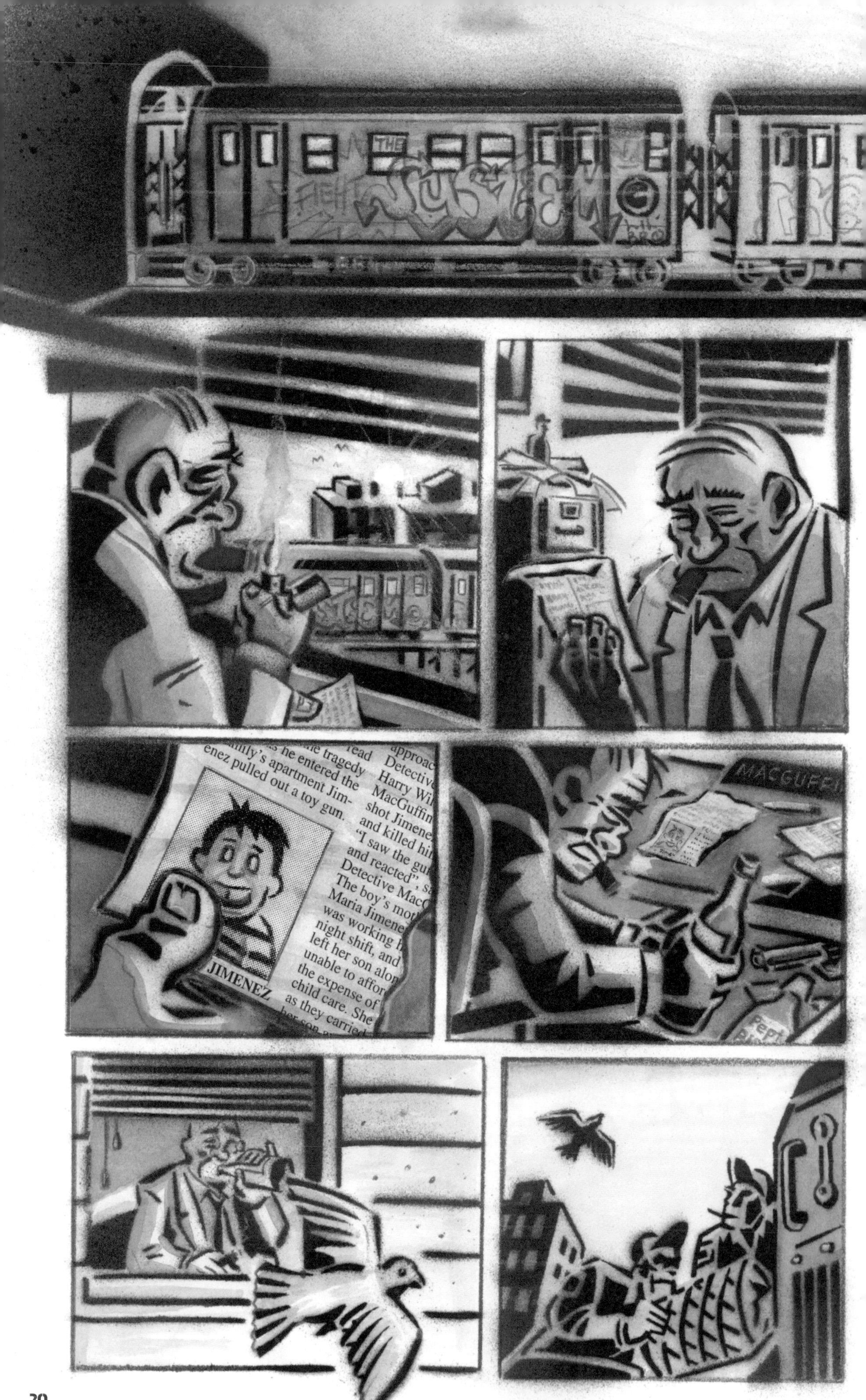
THE
read
he tragedy
s he entered the
mily's apartment Jim-
enez pulled out a toy gun.
approac
Detective
Harry Wi
MacGuffin
shot Jimene
and killed hi
"I saw the gu
and reacted", sa
Detective MacG
The boy's mot
Maria Jimene
was working
night shift, and
left her son alon
unable to affor
the expense of
child care. She
as they carried
JIMENEZ
MACGUFFI

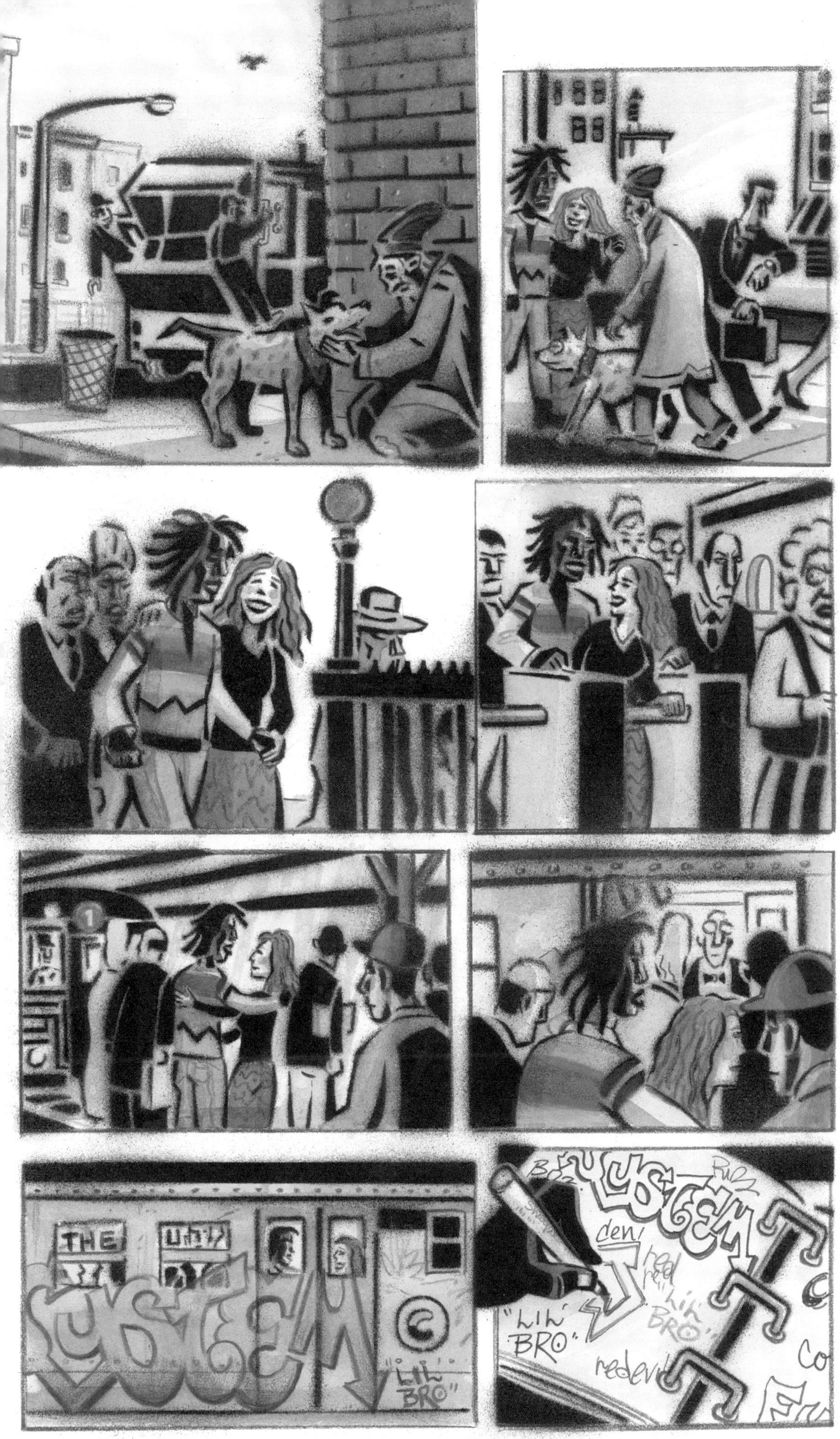
THE
"LIL' BRO"
"LIL' BRO"

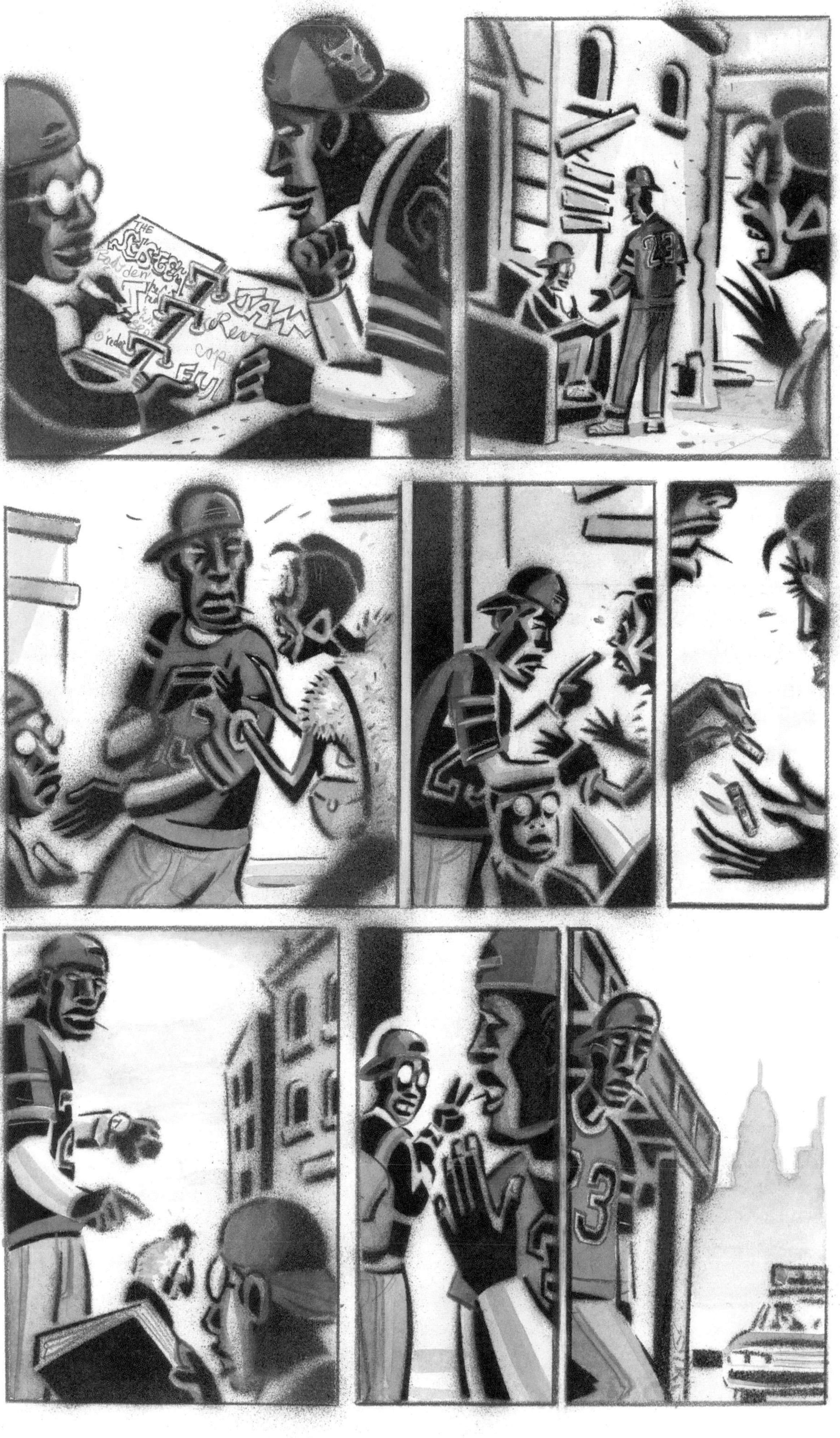

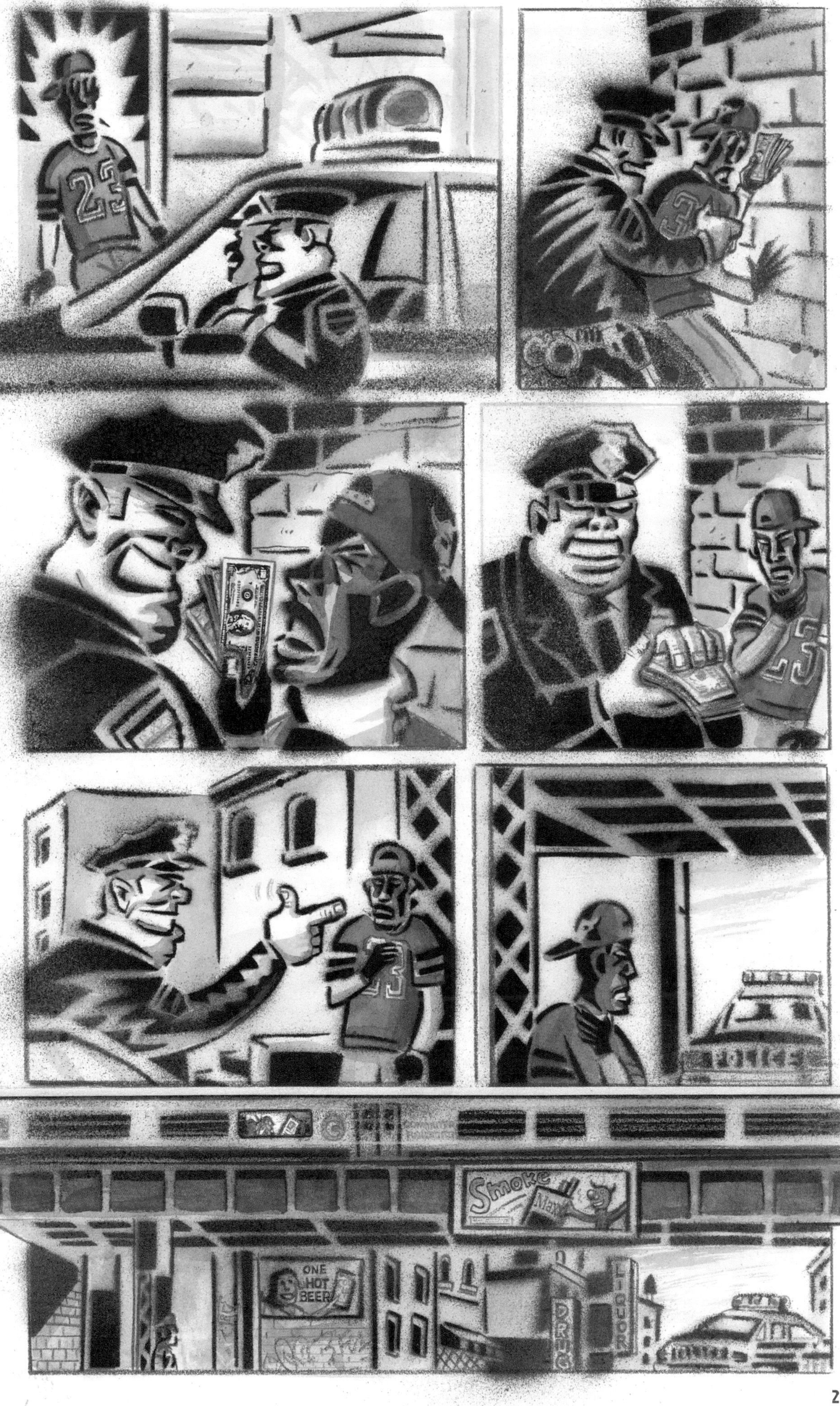
Smoke
Max
ONE
HOT
BEER
DRUG
LIQUOR

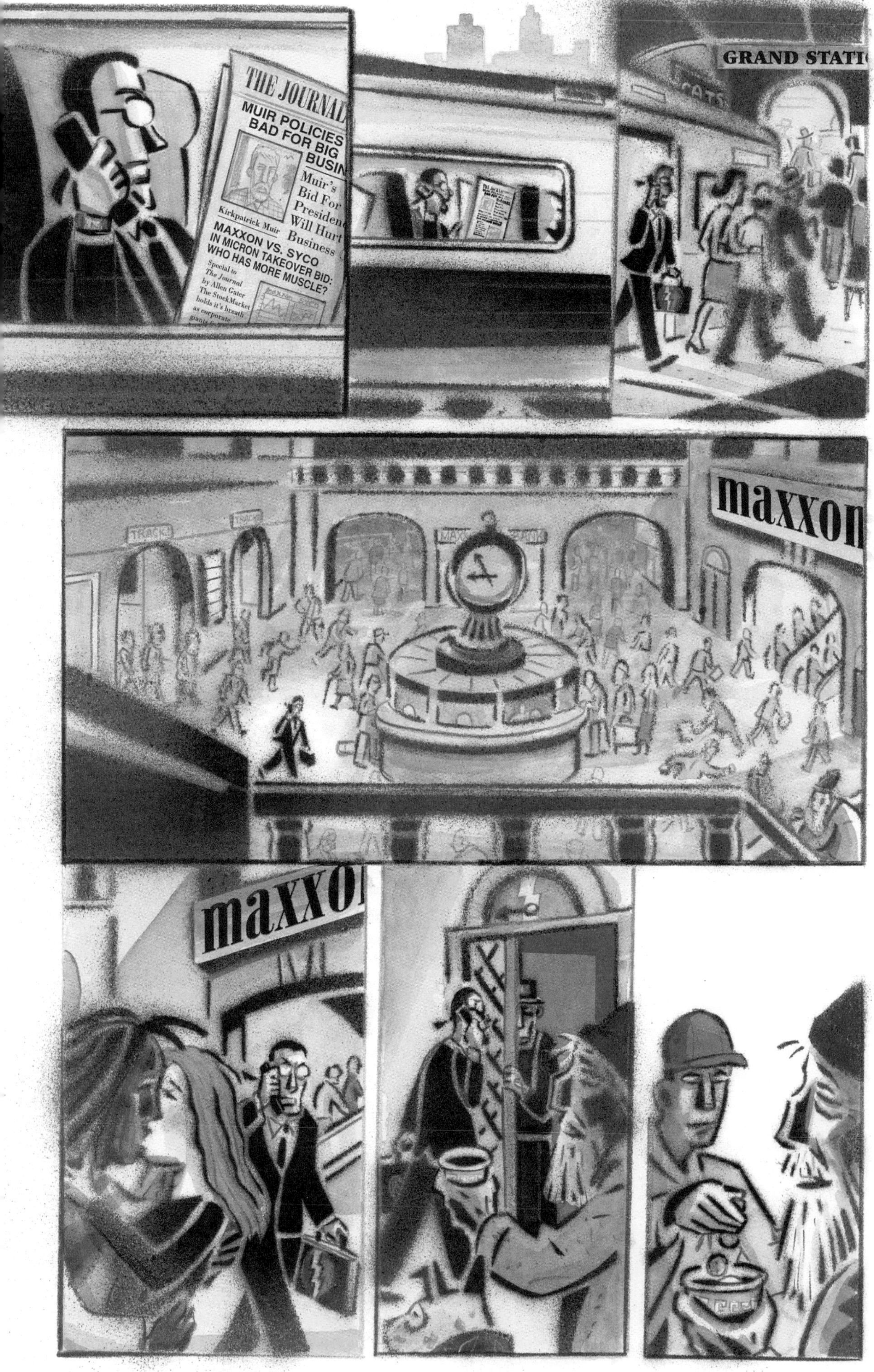
THE JOURNAL
MUIR POLICIES BAD FOR BIG BUSIN
Muir's Bid For Presiden Will Hurt Business
Kirkpatrick Muir
MAXXON VS. SYCO IN MICRON TAKEOVER BID: WHO HAS MORE MUSCLE?
Special to The Journal by Allen Gater
The StockMarket holds it's breath as corporate
GRAND STATI
maxxon
maxxo

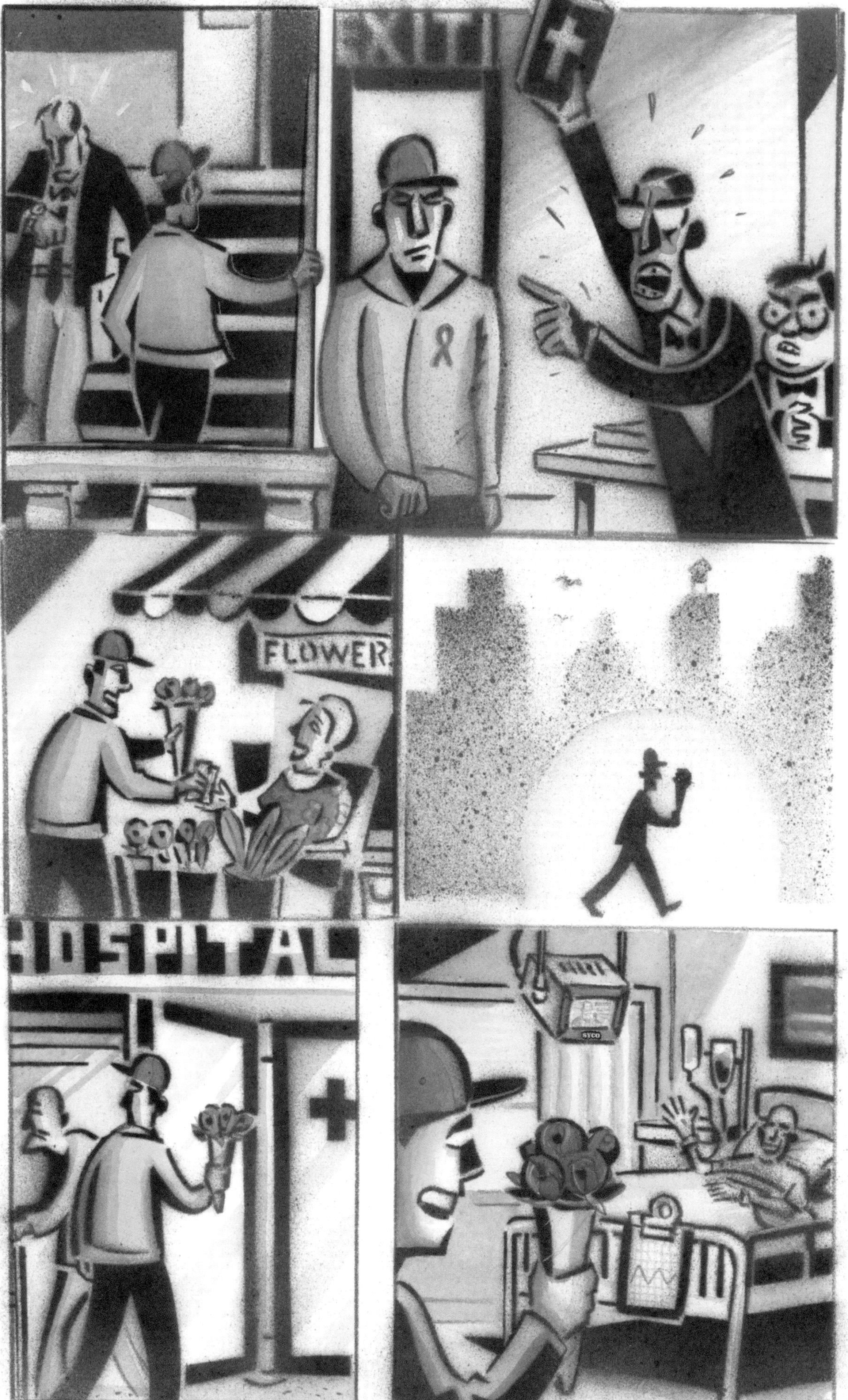
FLOWER
SYCO

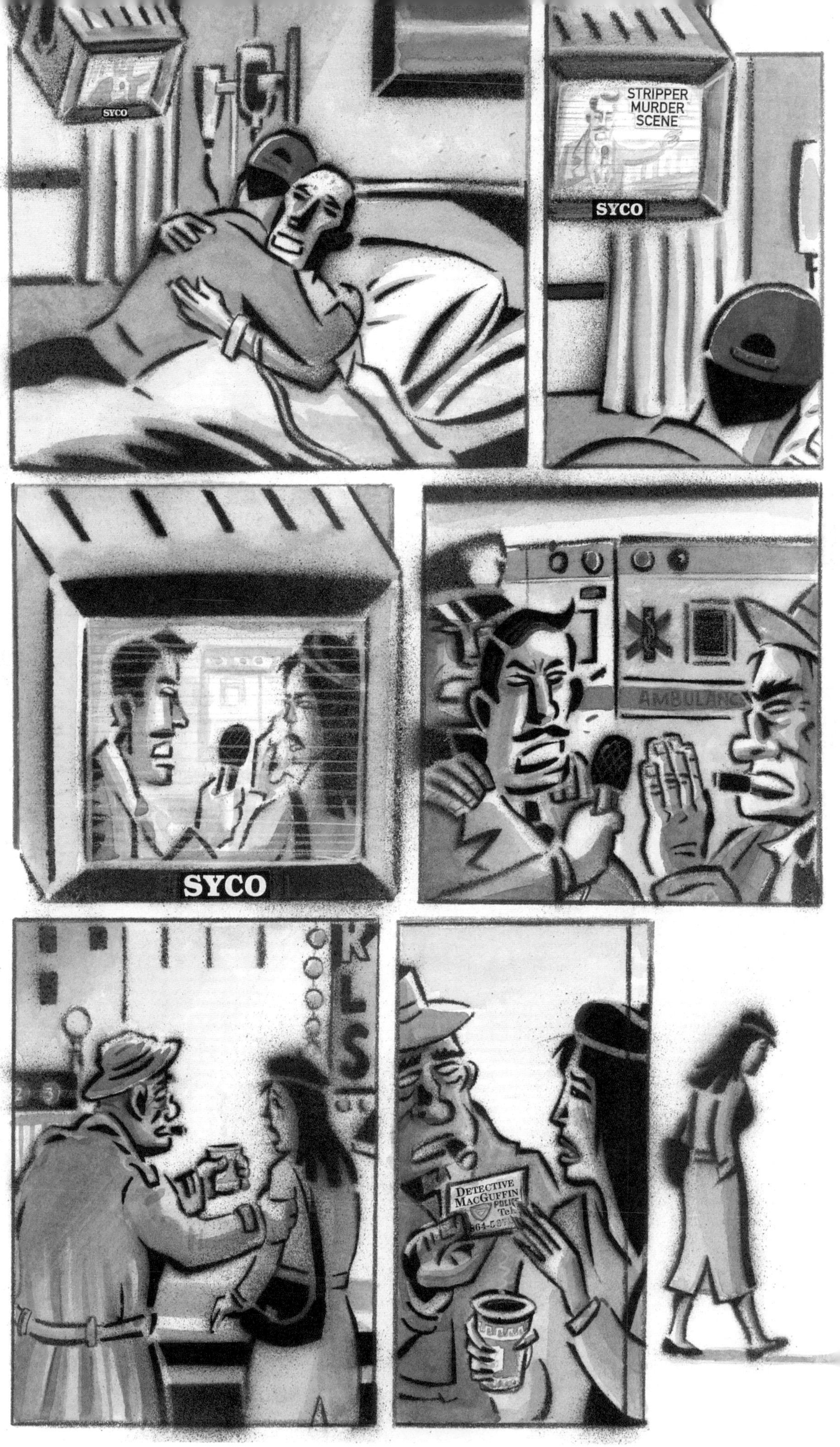
SYCO
STRIPPER MURDER SCENE
SYCO
SYCO
DETECTIVE MacGUFFIN

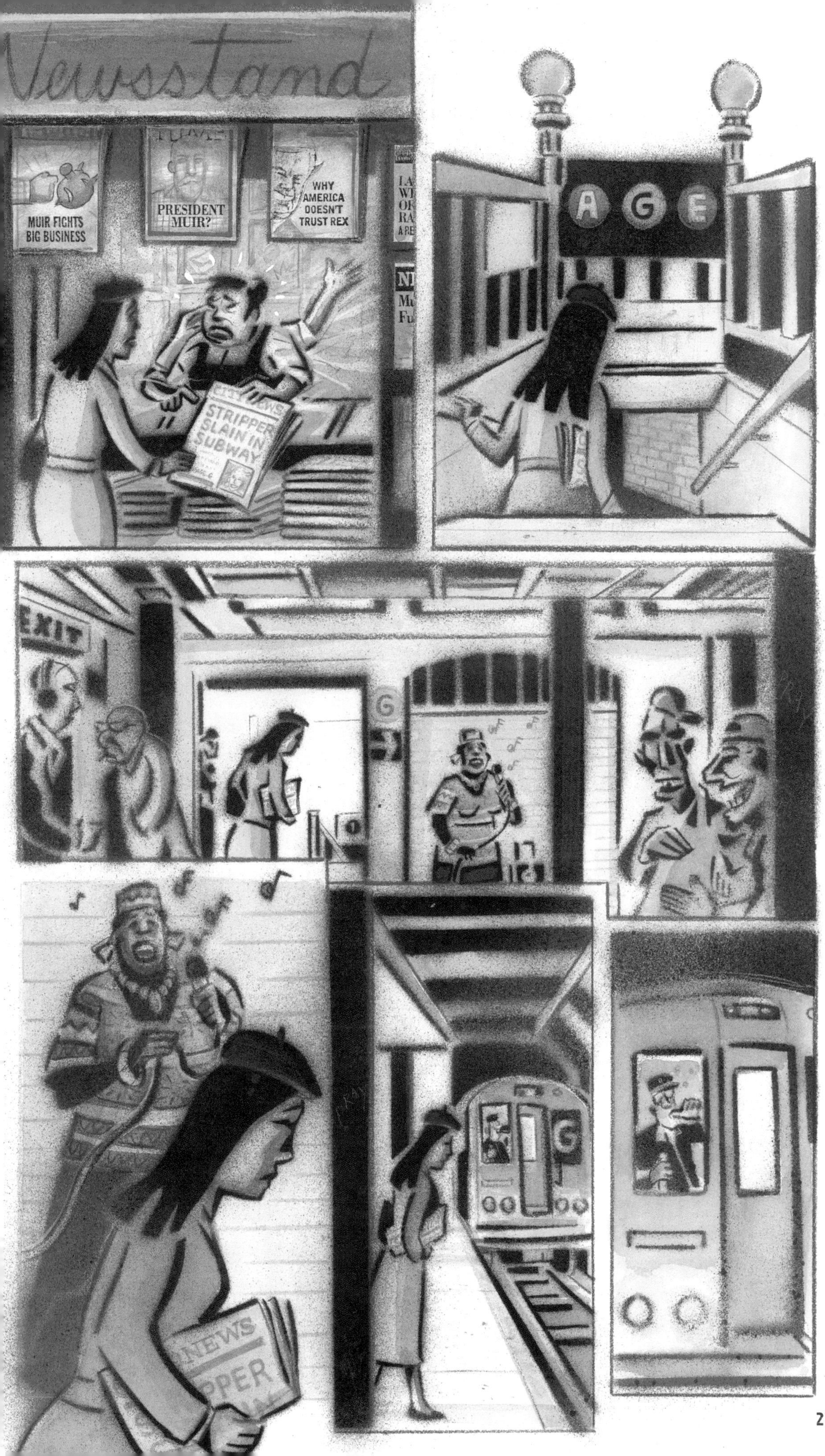
Newsstand
MUIR FIGHTS BIG BUSINESS
PRESIDENT MUIR?
WHY AMERICA DOESN'T TRUST REX
STRIPPER SLAIN IN SUBWAY
A G E
EXIT
G
NEWS

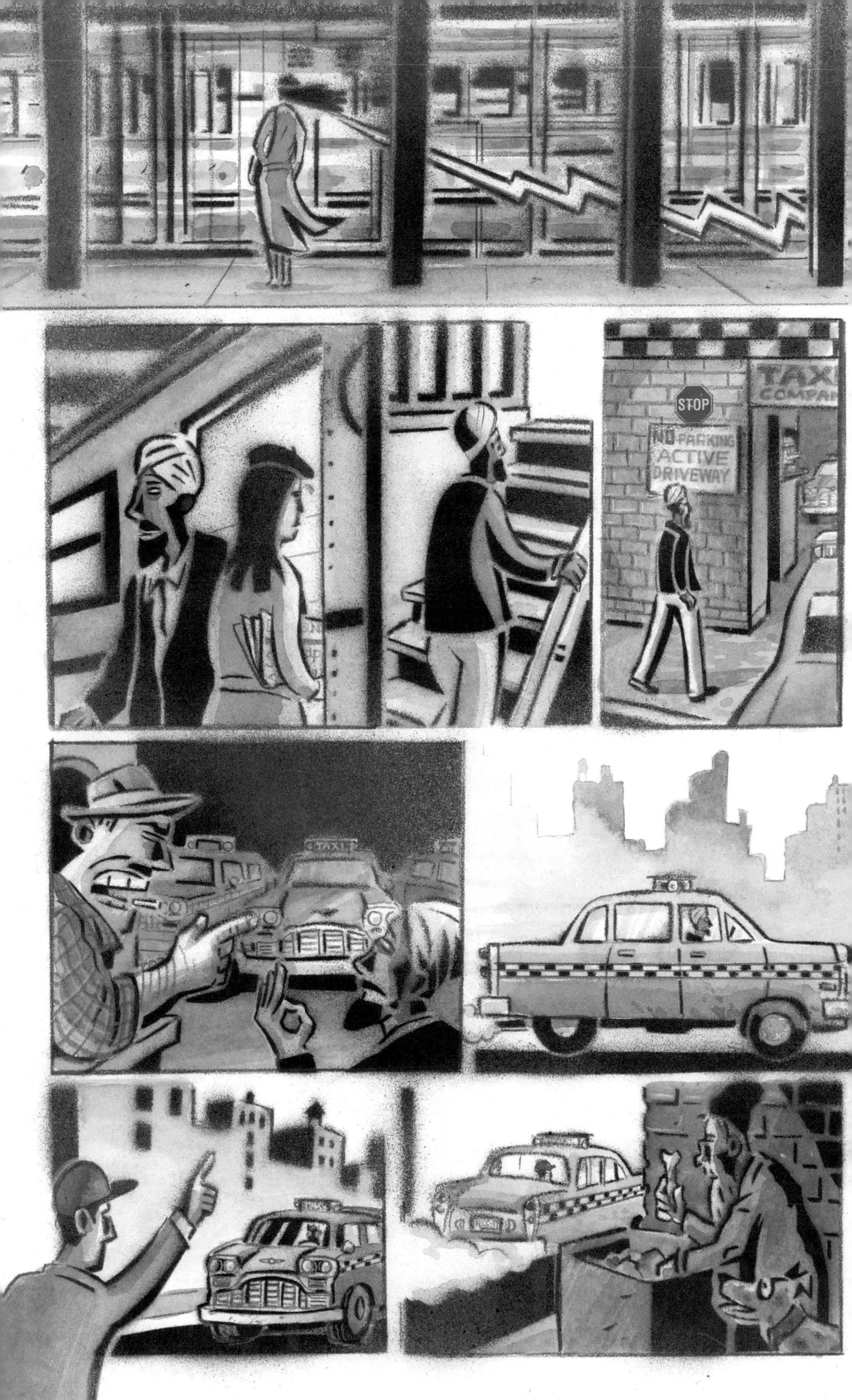
STOP
NO PARKING
ACTIVE
DRIVEWAY
TAXI

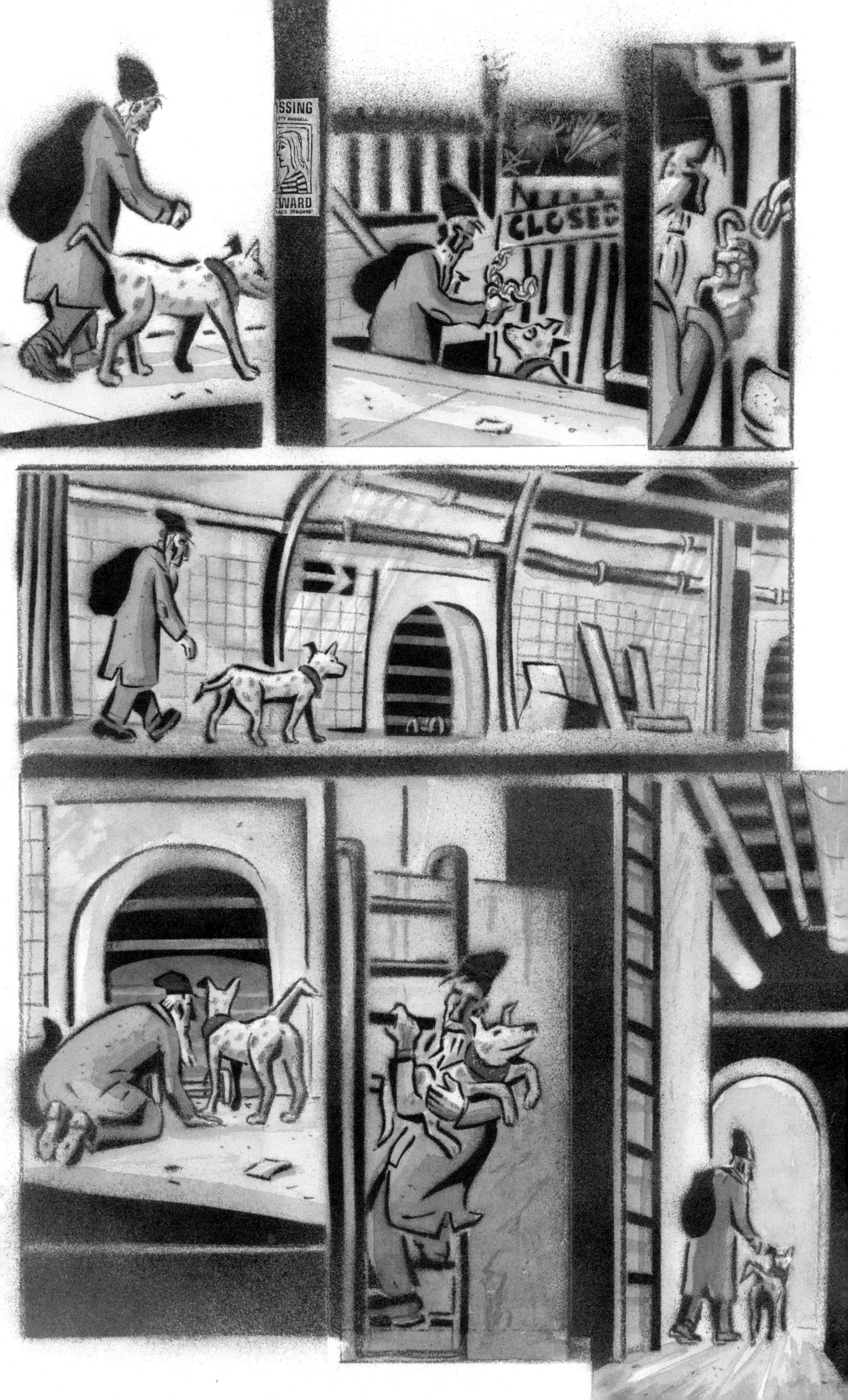
SSING
EWARD
CLOSED

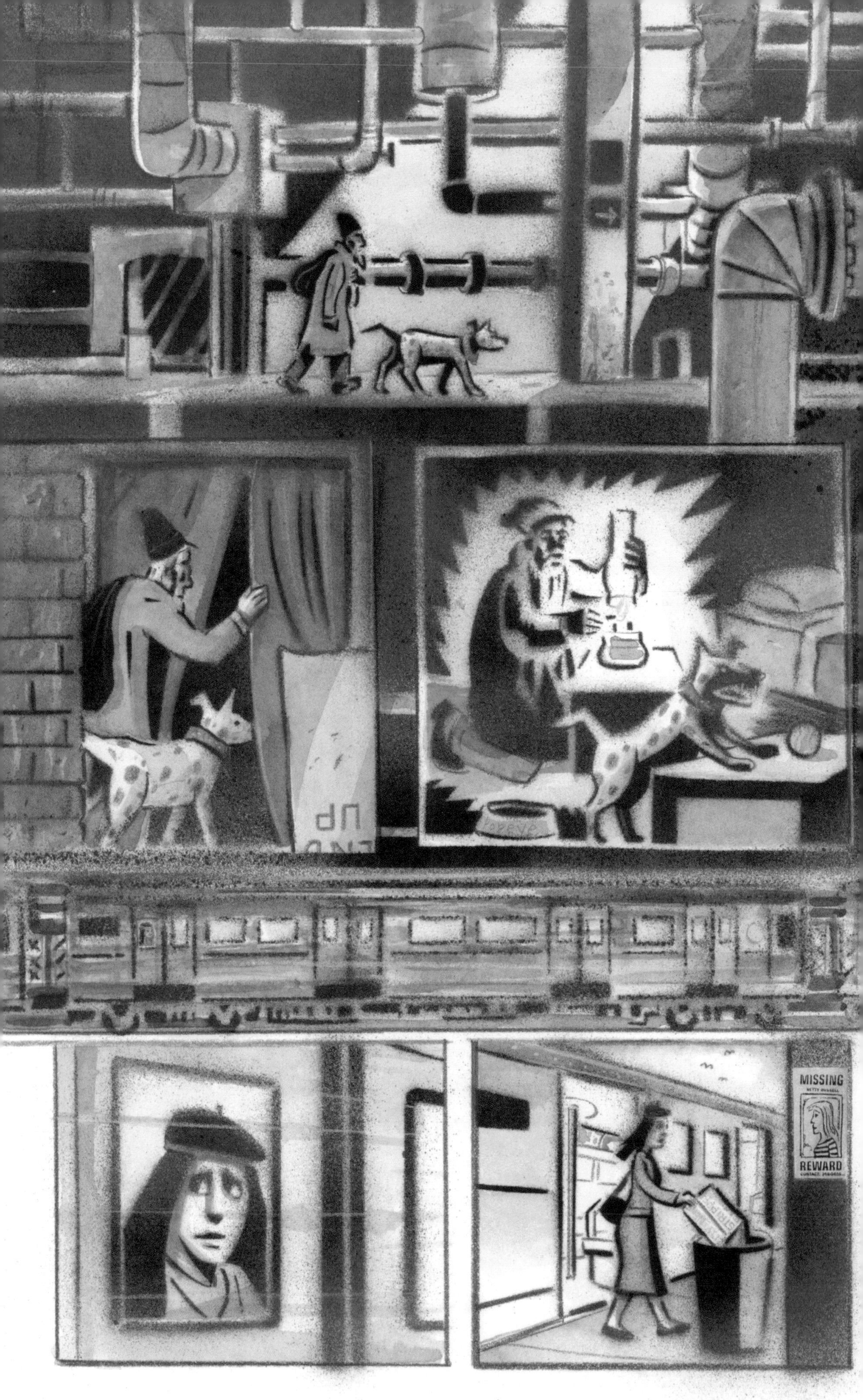
MISSING
REWARD

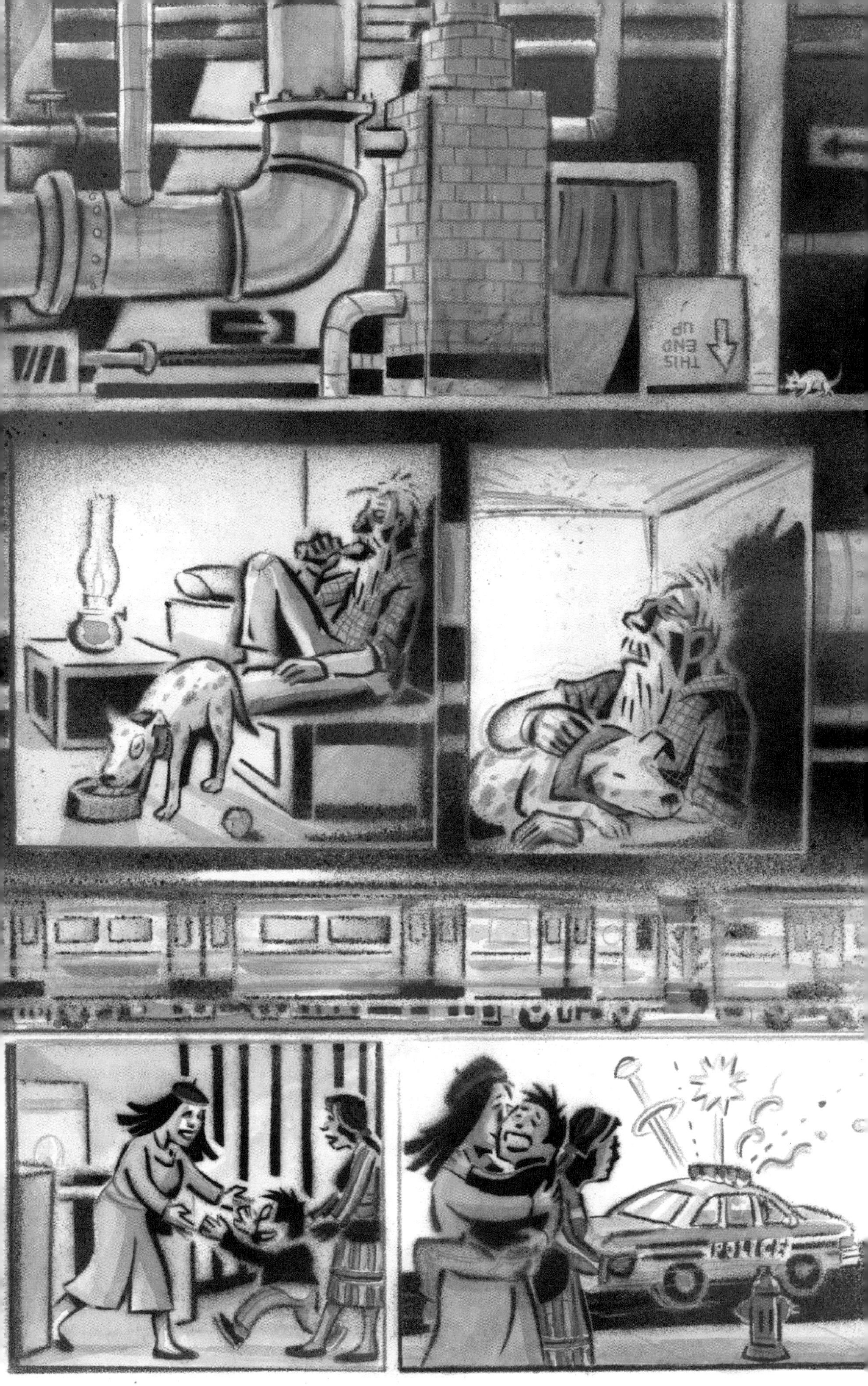
THIS END UP
POLICE

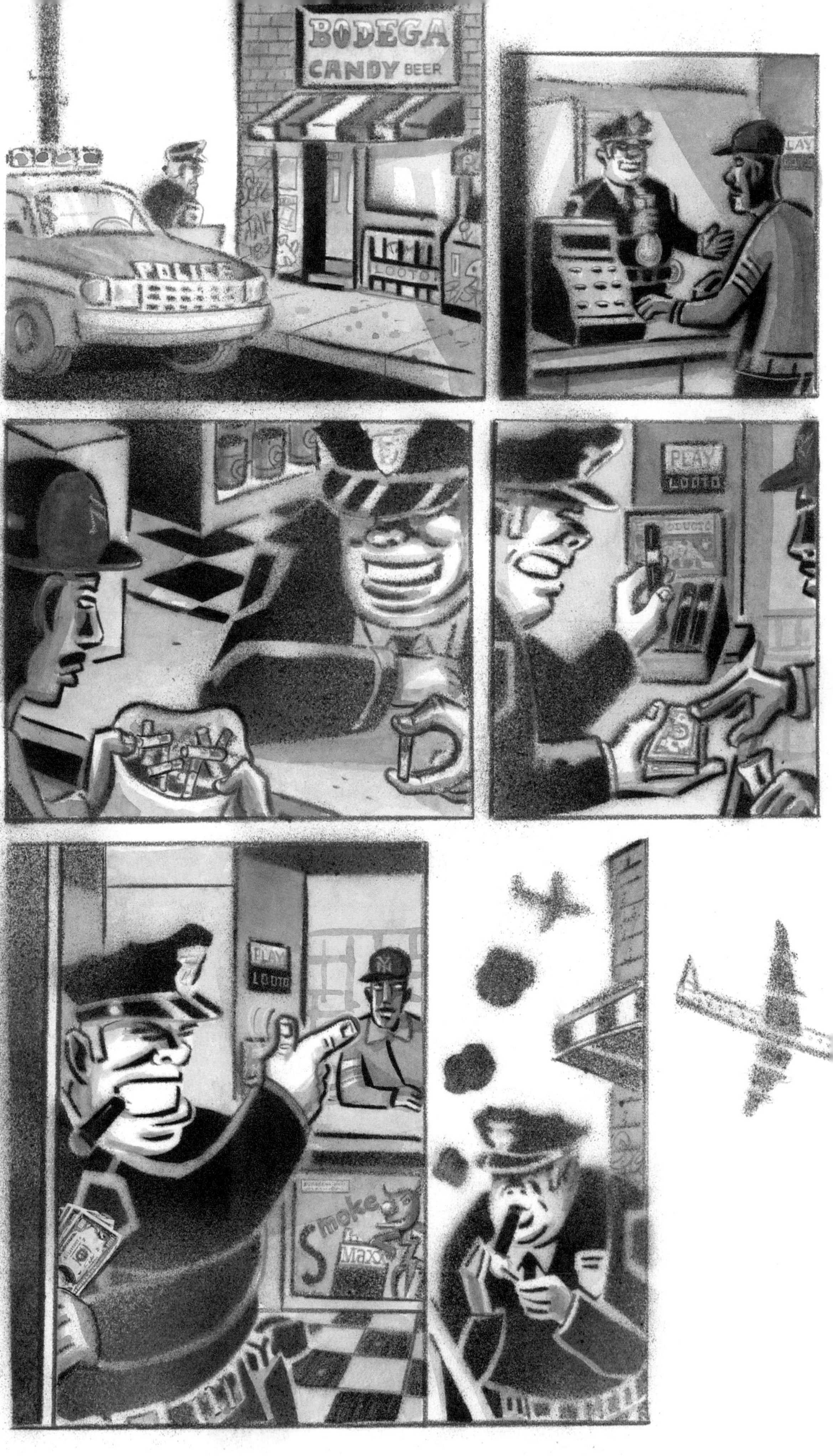
BODEGA
CANDY BEER
POLICE
LOTTO
PLAY
LOTTO
PLAY
LOTTO
Smoke

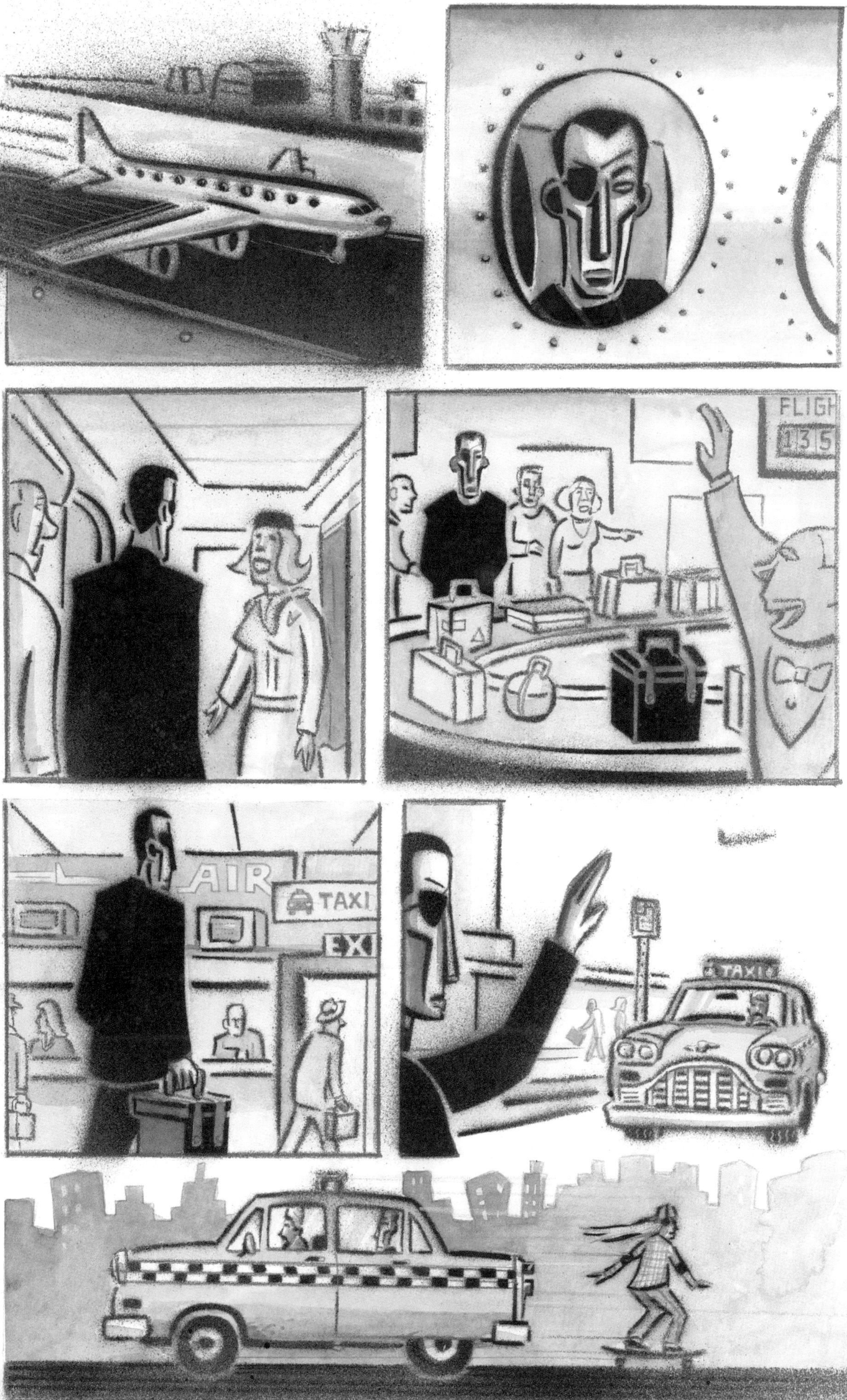
FLIGH
135
AIR
TAXI
EXI
TAXI

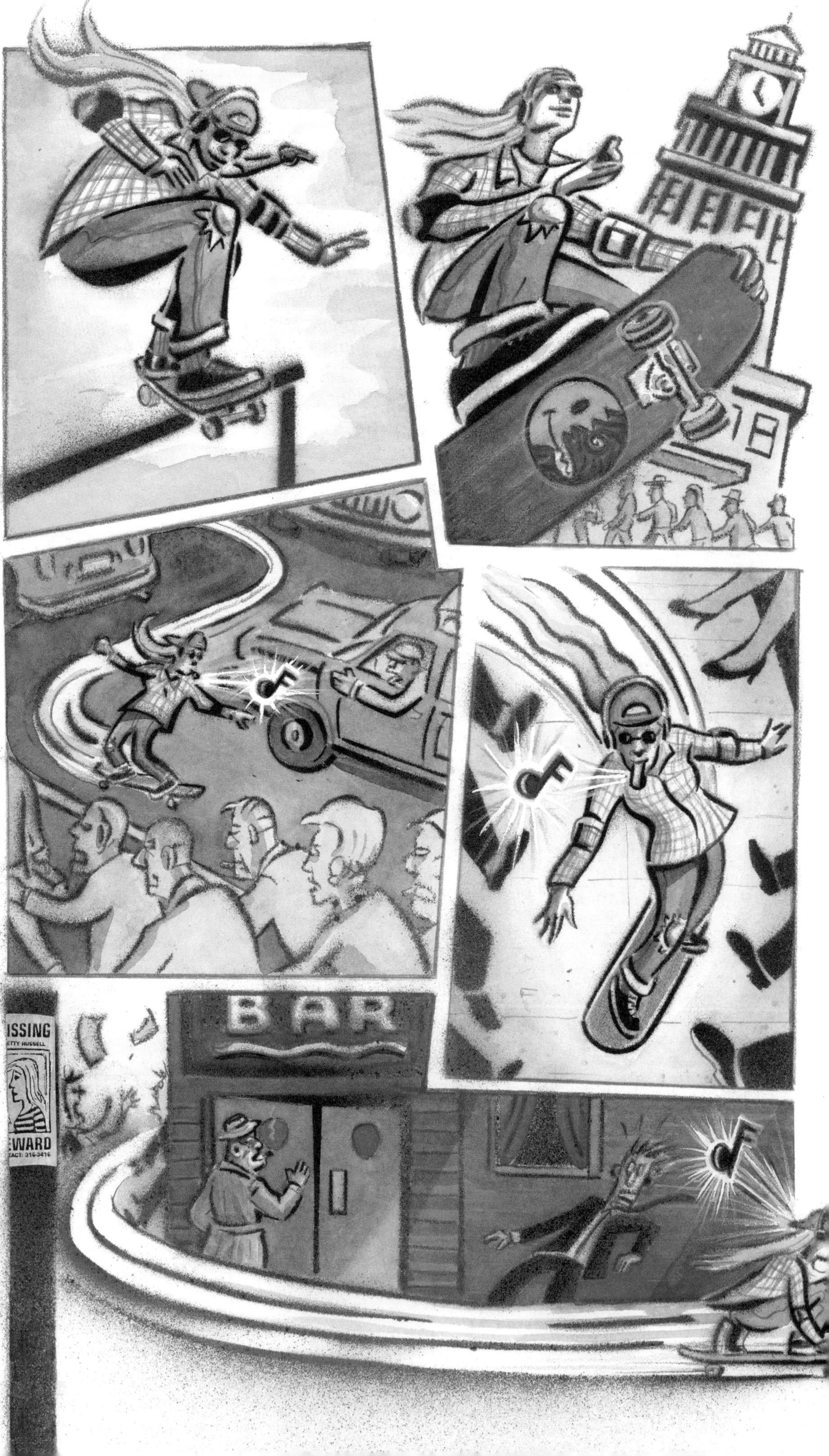

BAR
ISSING
ETTY RUSSELL
EWARD
TACT: 316-3416

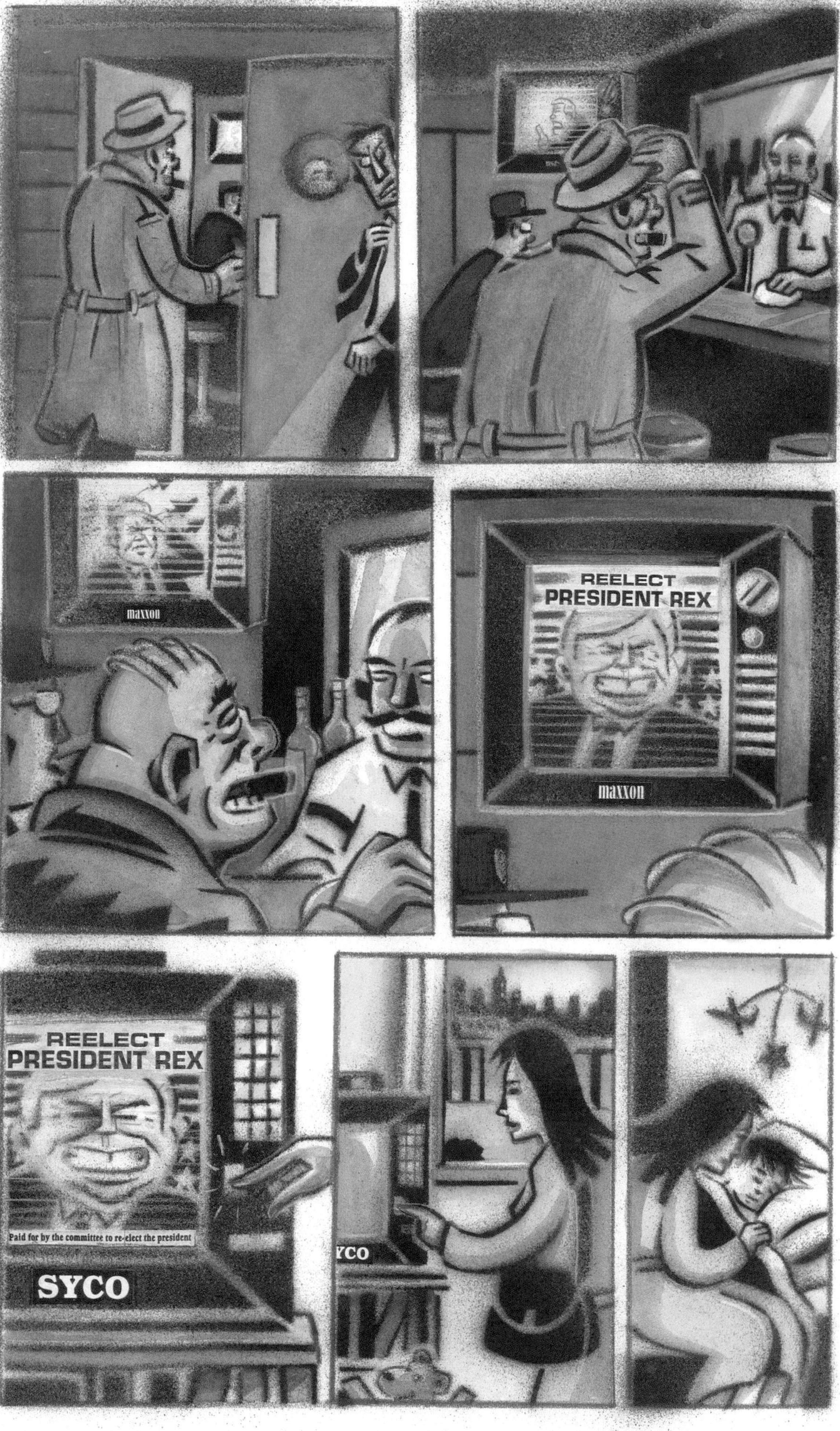
maxxon
REELECT
PRESIDENT REX
maxxon
REELECT
PRESIDENT REX
Paid for by the committee to re-elect the president
SYCO
YCO

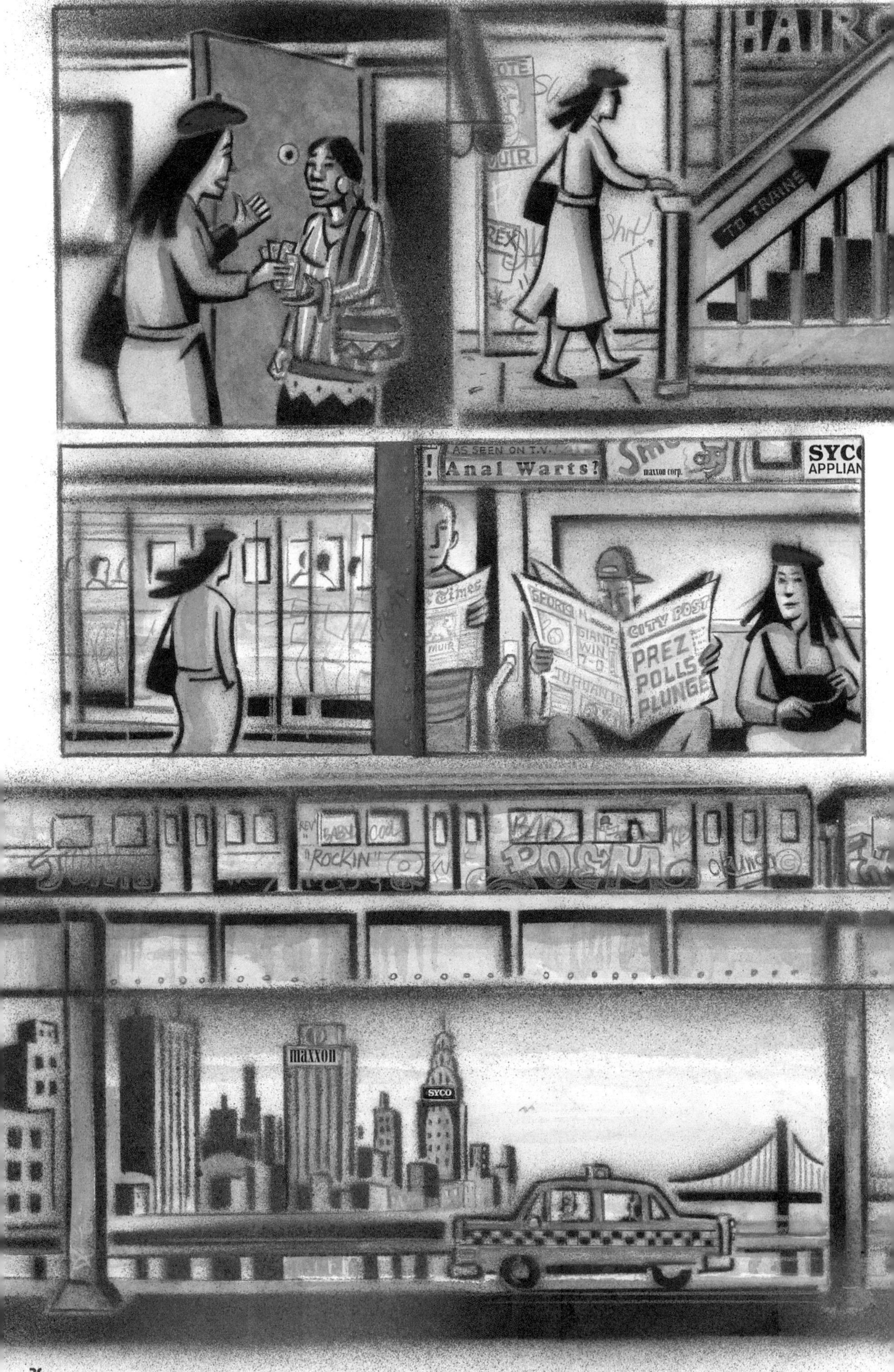
HAIR
VOTE
MUIR
REX
TO TRAINS
AS SEEN ON T.V.
Anal Warts?
maxxon corp.
SYCO
APPLIAN
MUIR
CITY POST
GIANTS WIN 7-0
PREZ POLLS PLUNGE
BABY
"ROCKIN"
BAD
maxxon
SYCO

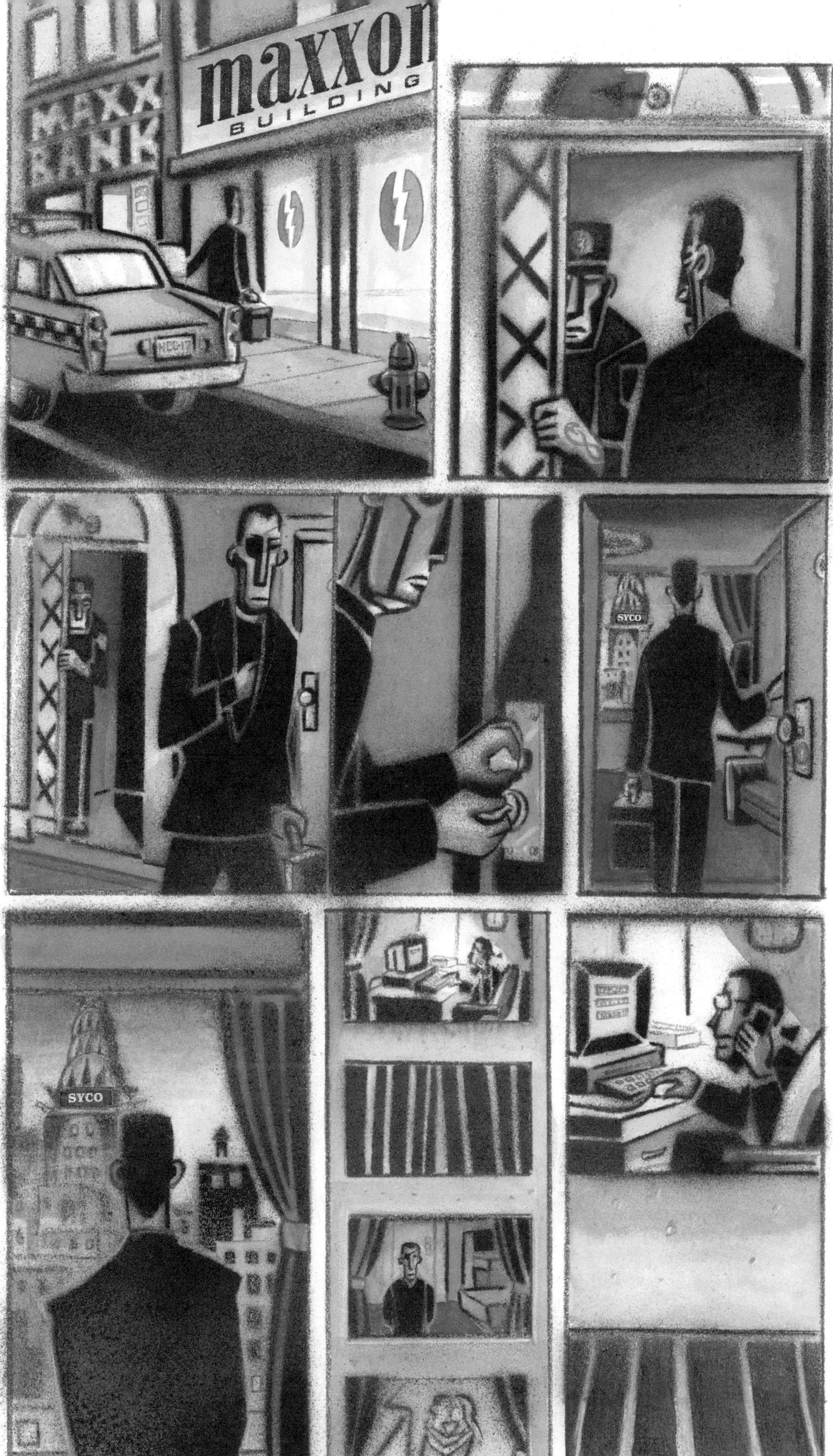
maxxon
BUILDING
MAXX
BANK
SYCO
SYCO

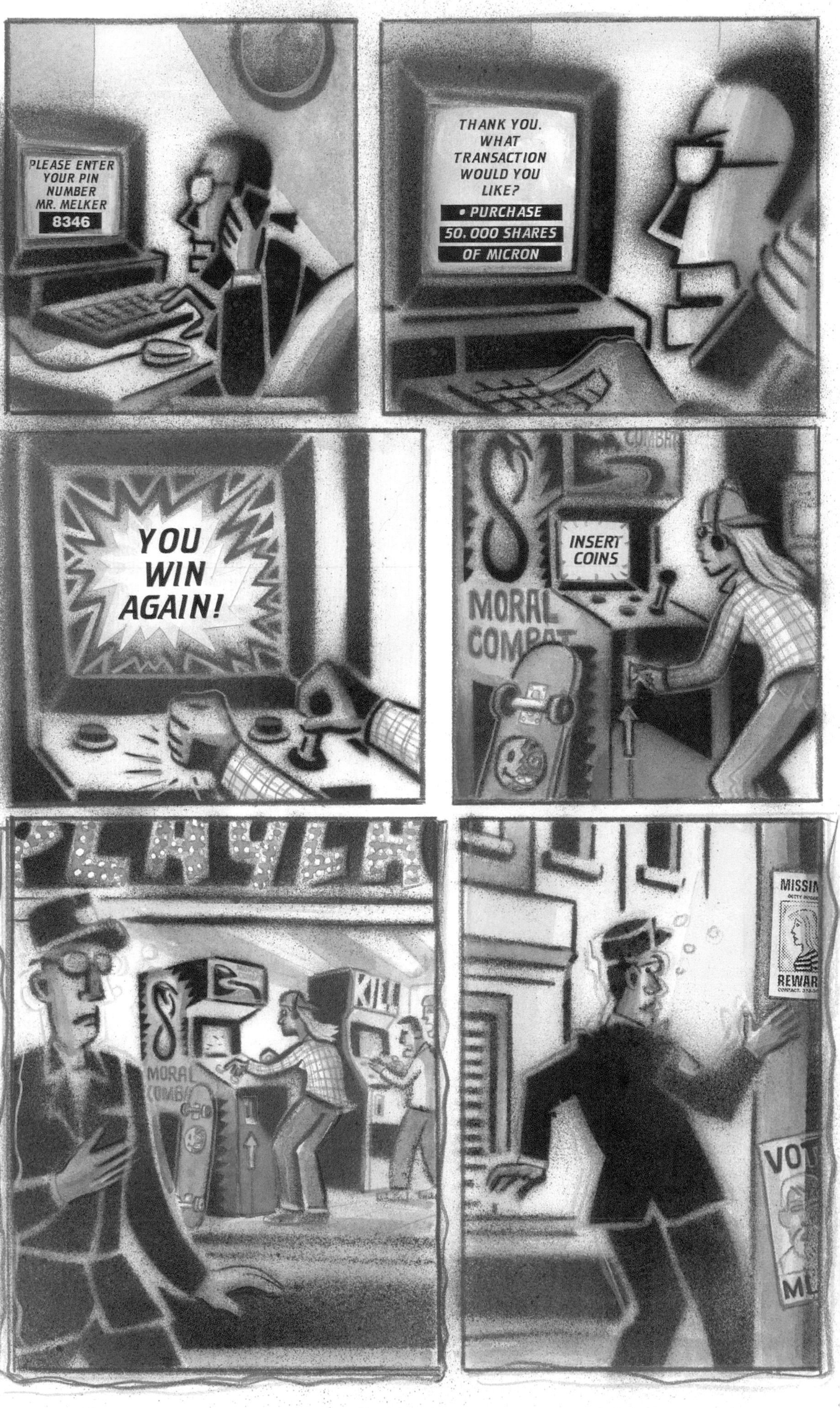
PLEASE ENTER YOUR PIN NUMBER MR. MELKER
8346
THANK YOU. WHAT TRANSACTION WOULD YOU LIKE?
• PURCHASE
50,000 SHARES
OF MICRON
YOU WIN AGAIN!
INSERT COINS
MORAL

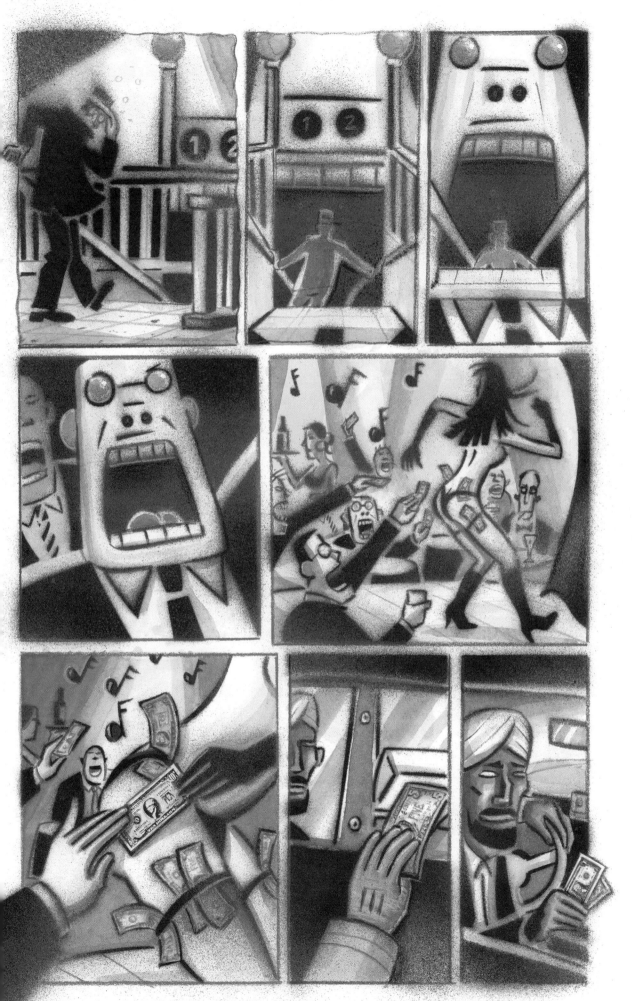

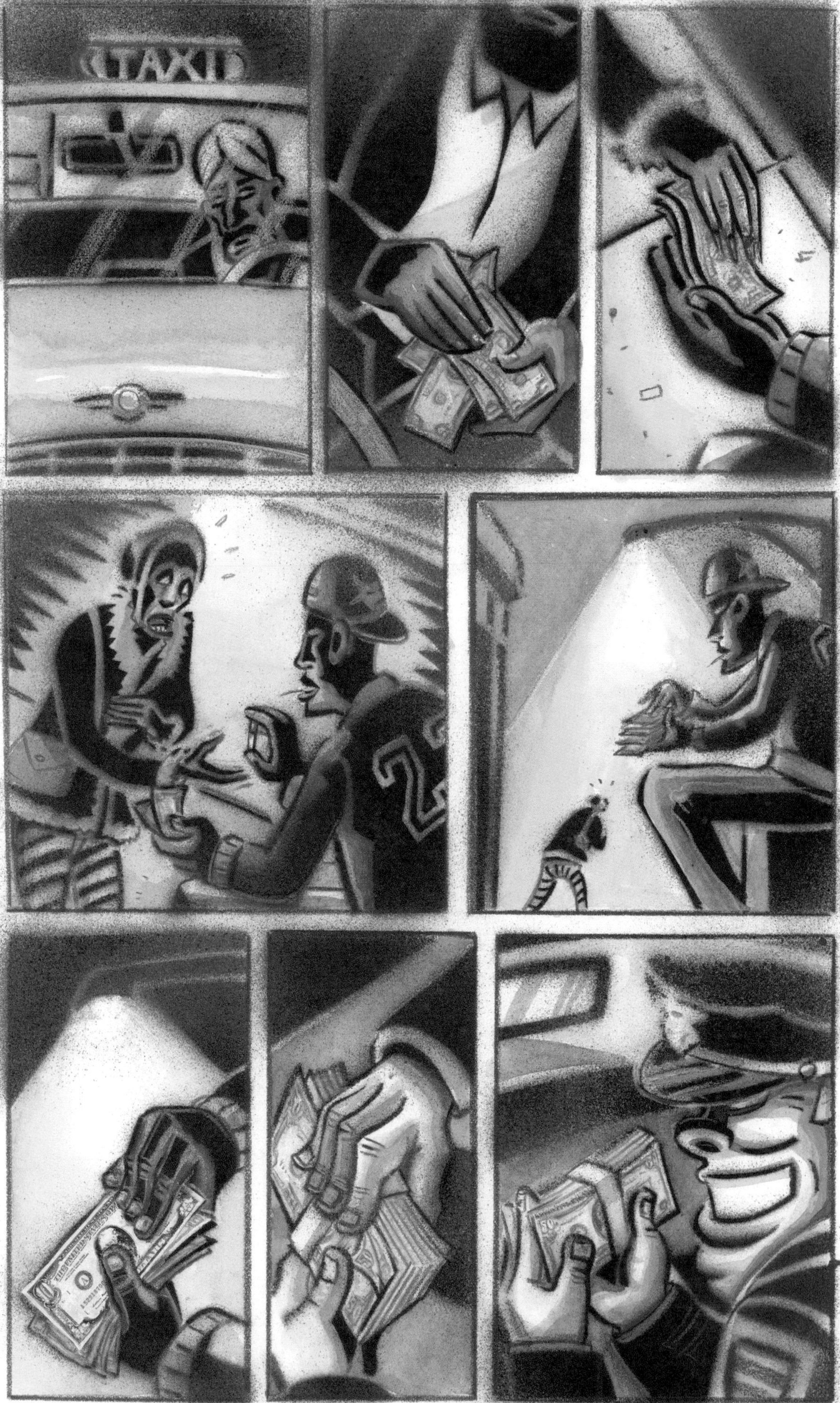
TAXI

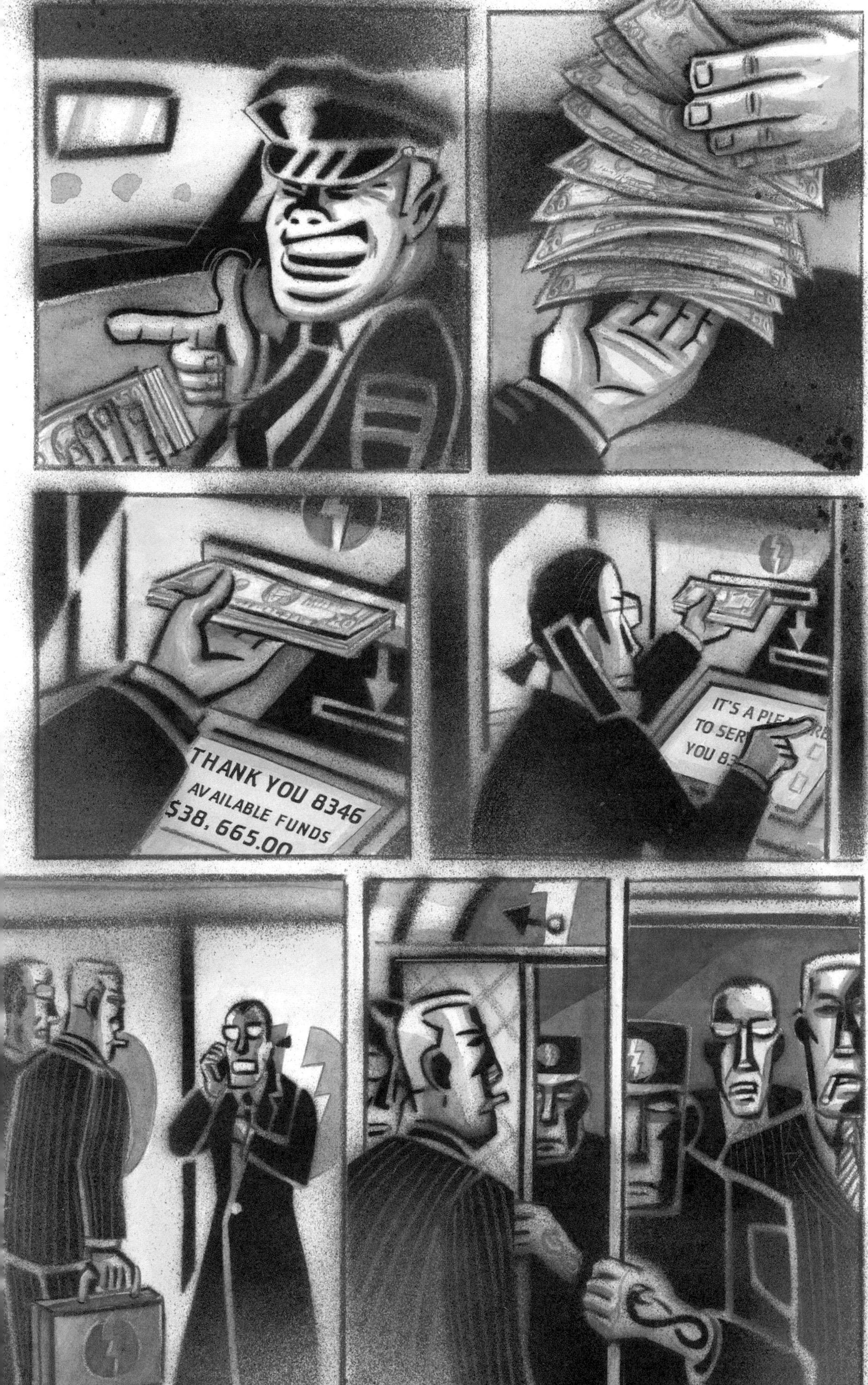
THANK YOU 8346
AVAILABLE FUNDS
$38, 665.00
IT'S A PLEA
TO SER
YOU 83

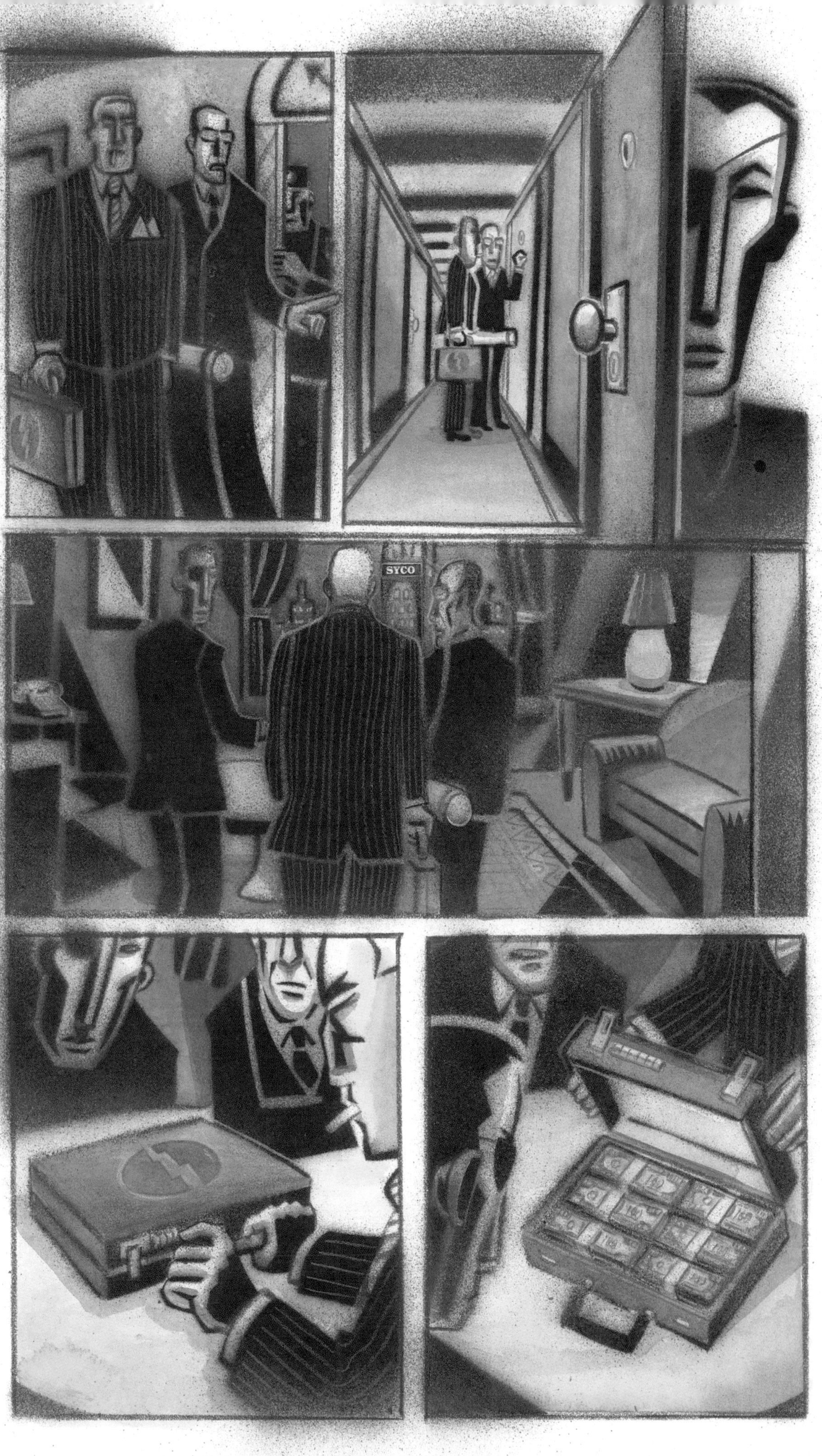
SYCO

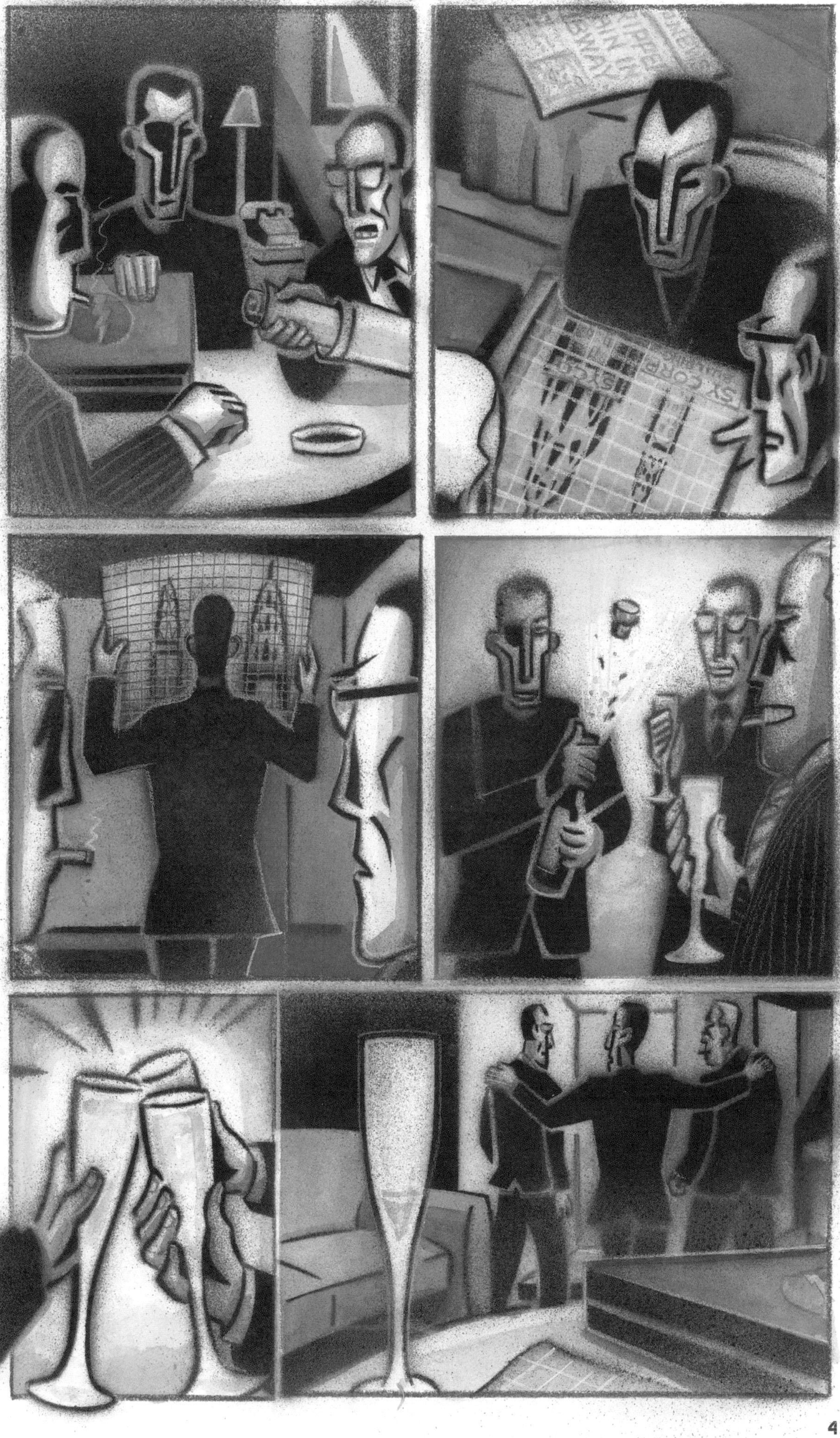
SY CORP

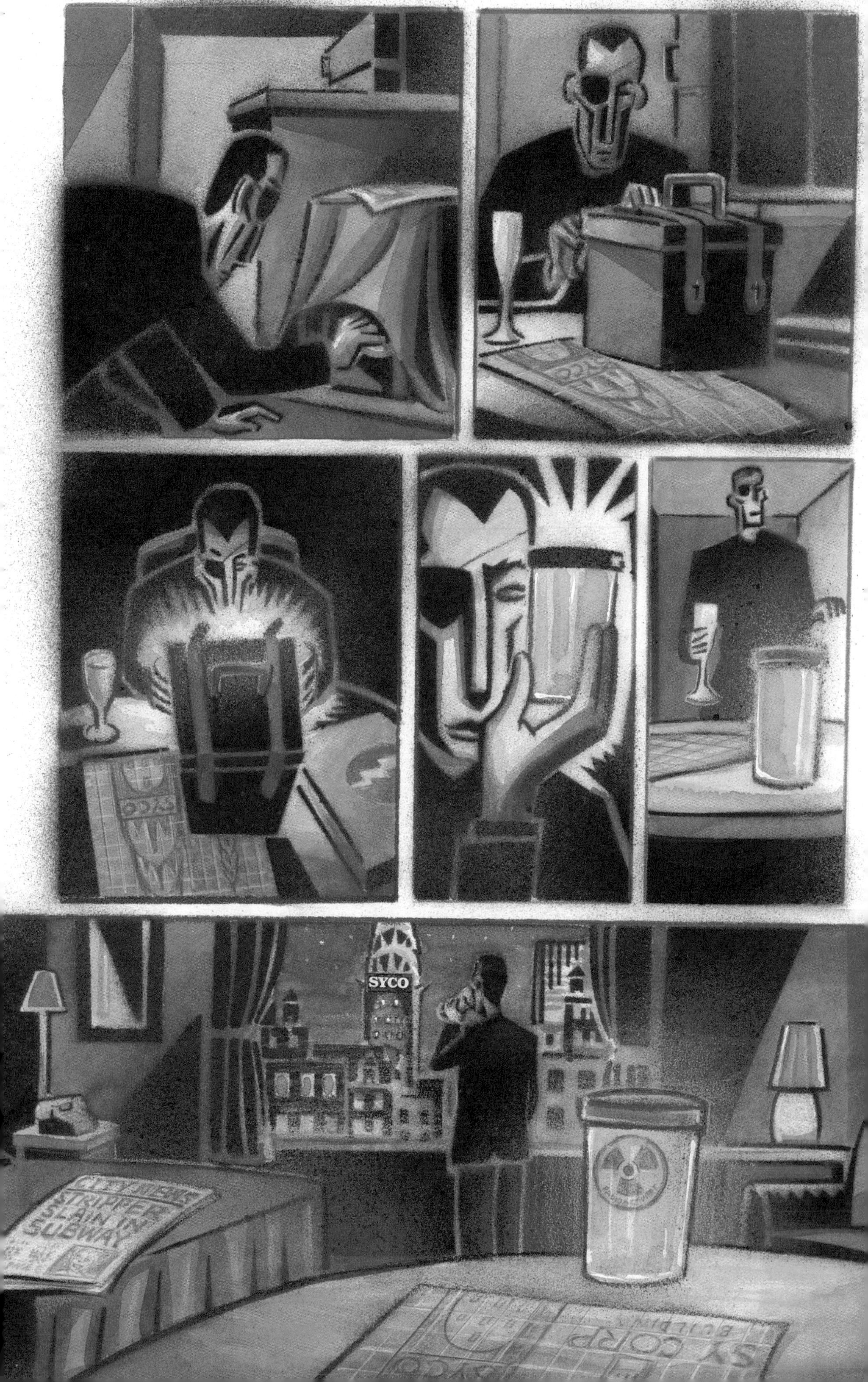
SYCO
CITY NEWS
STRIPPER SLAIN IN SUBWAY
SYCORP BUILDING

"Who sees with equal eye, as God of all,
A hero perish or a sparrow fall,
Atoms or systems into ruin hurl'd,
And now a bubble burst, and now a world."

—ALEXANDER POPE

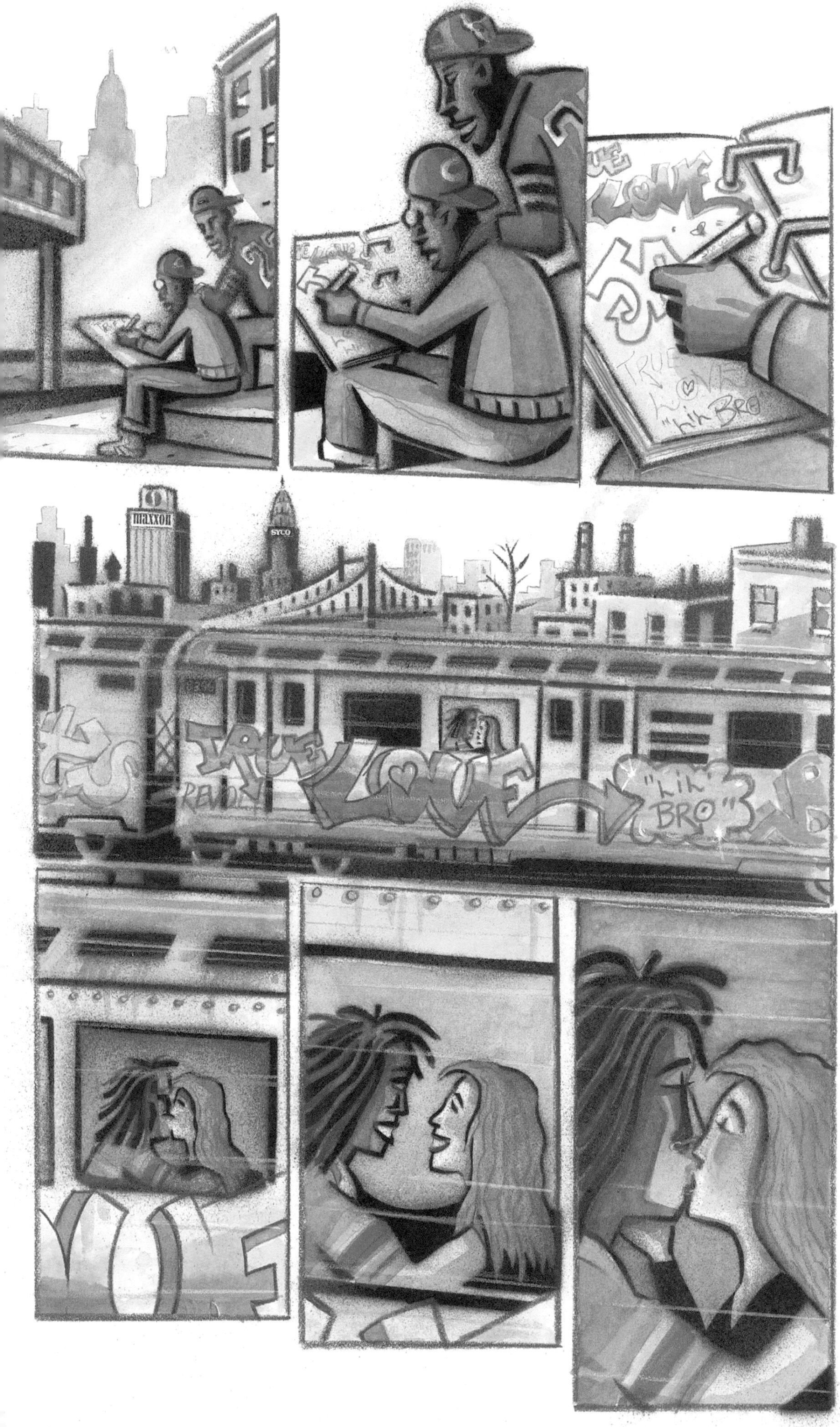
maxxon
SYCO
TRUE LOVE
"Lil' BRO"

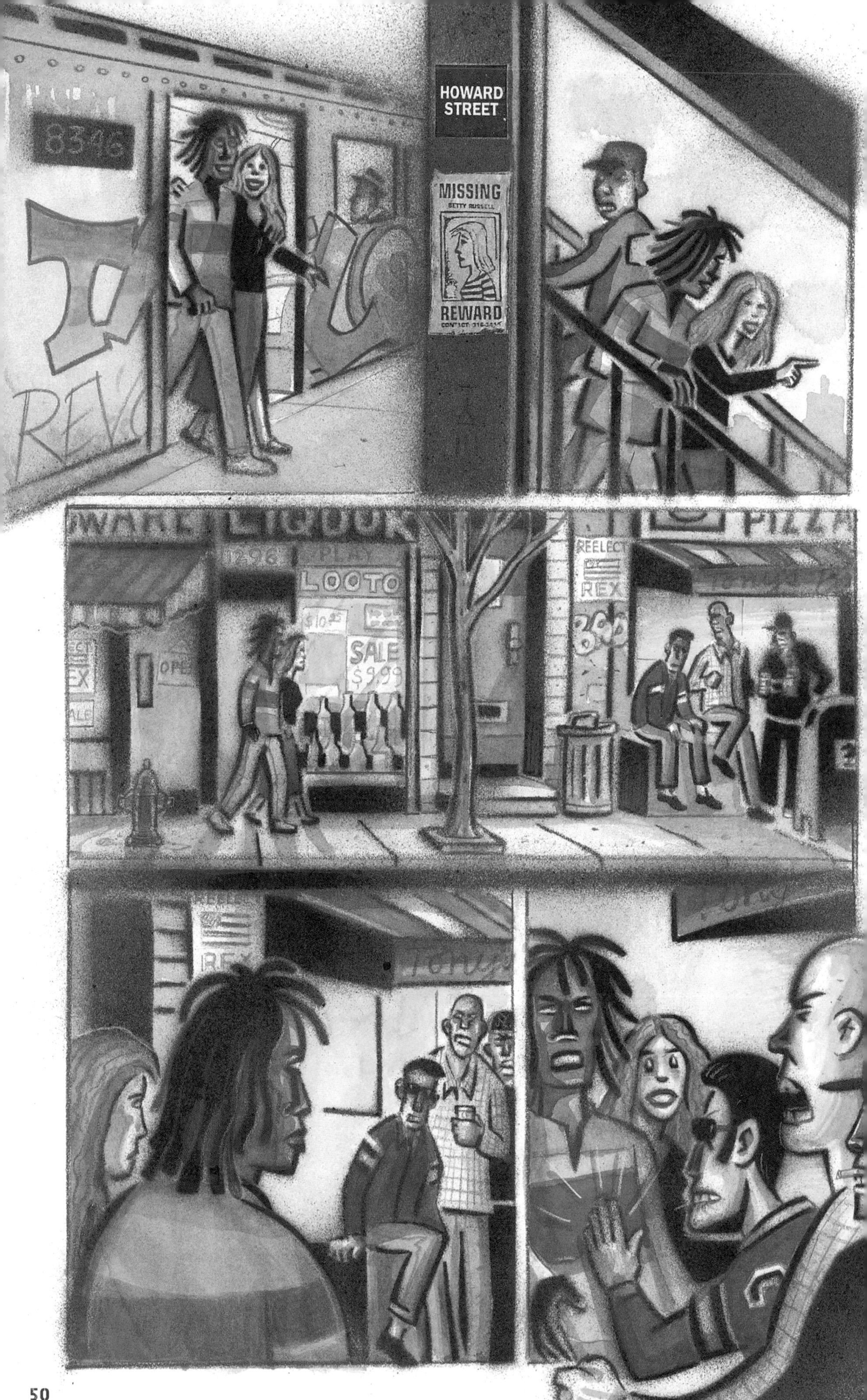
8346
HOWARD STREET
MISSING
BETTY RUSSELL
REWARD
LIQUOR
1296
PLAY
LOOTO
SALE $9.99
REELECT REX
PIZZA

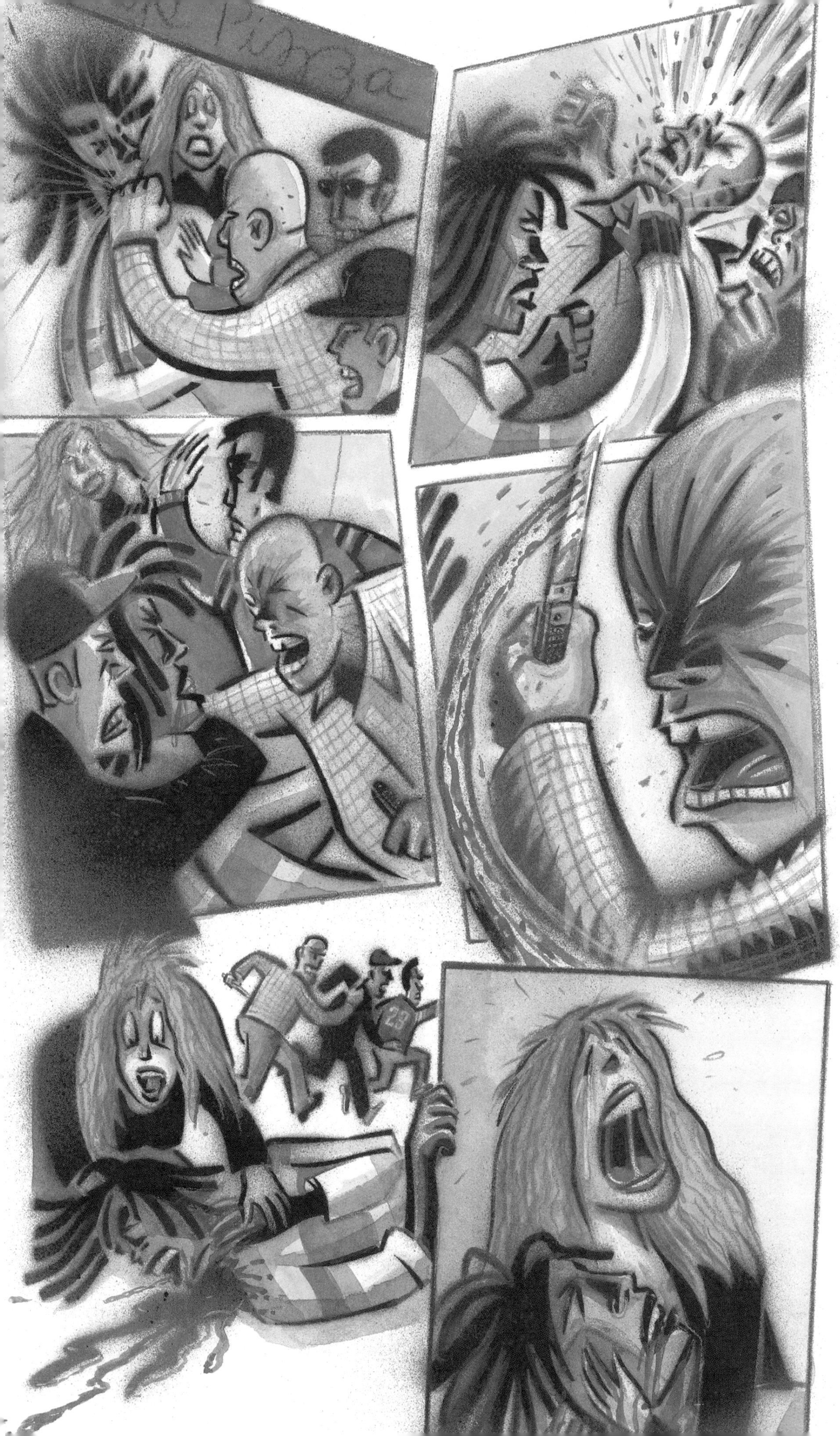

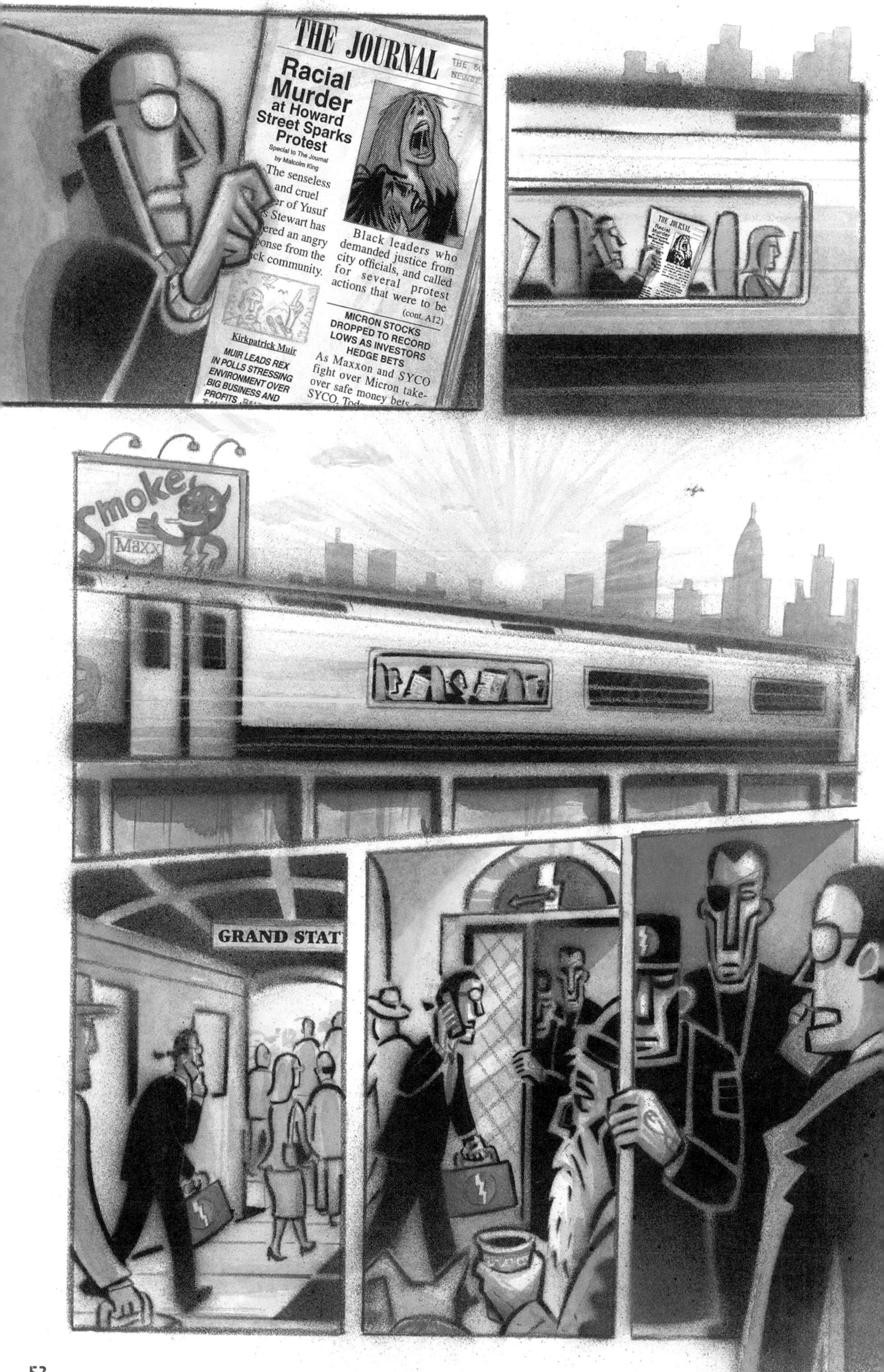
THE JOURNAL
Racial Murder at Howard Street Sparks Protest
Special to The Journal
by Malcolm King
The senseless and cruel
er of Yusuf
s Stewart has
ered an angry
ponse from the
ck community.
Black leaders who demanded justice from city officials, and called for several protest actions that were to be
(cont. A12)
Kirkpatrick Muir
MUIR LEADS REX IN POLLS STRESSING ENVIRONMENT OVER BIG BUSINESS AND PROFITS
MICRON STOCKS DROPPED TO RECORD LOWS AS INVESTORS HEDGE BETS
As Maxxon and SYCO fight over Micron take- over safe money bets
Smoke
Maxx
GRAND STAT

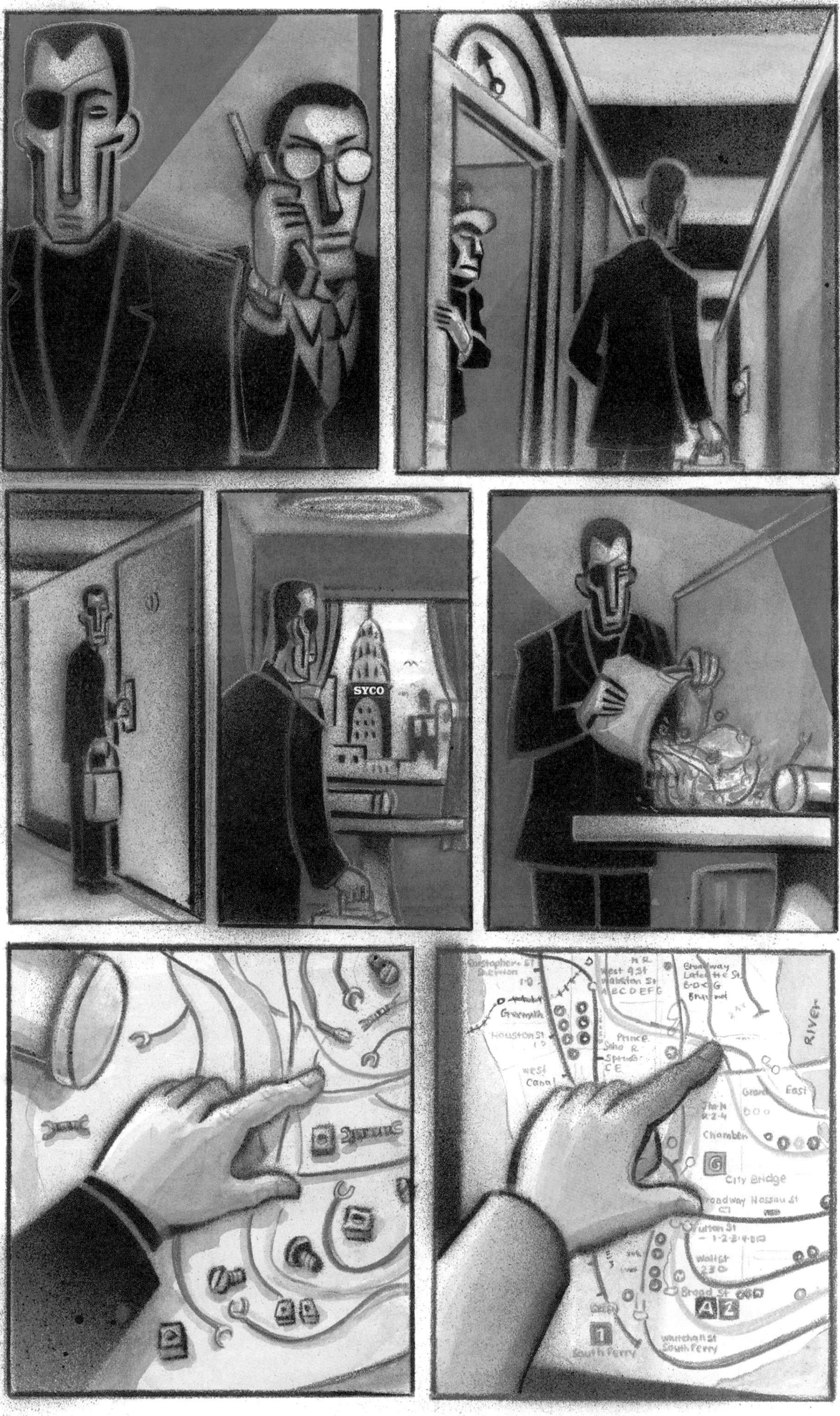
SYCO
Christopher St
West 4 St
Washington Sq
A B C D E F G
Broadway
Lafayette St
B-D-F-G
Greenwich
Houston St
Prince
Soho
Spring
C E
West
Canal
RIVER
Grand
East
Chamber
City Bridge
Broadway Nassau St
Fulton St
Wall St
Broad St
A Z
1
South Ferry
Whitehall St
South Ferry

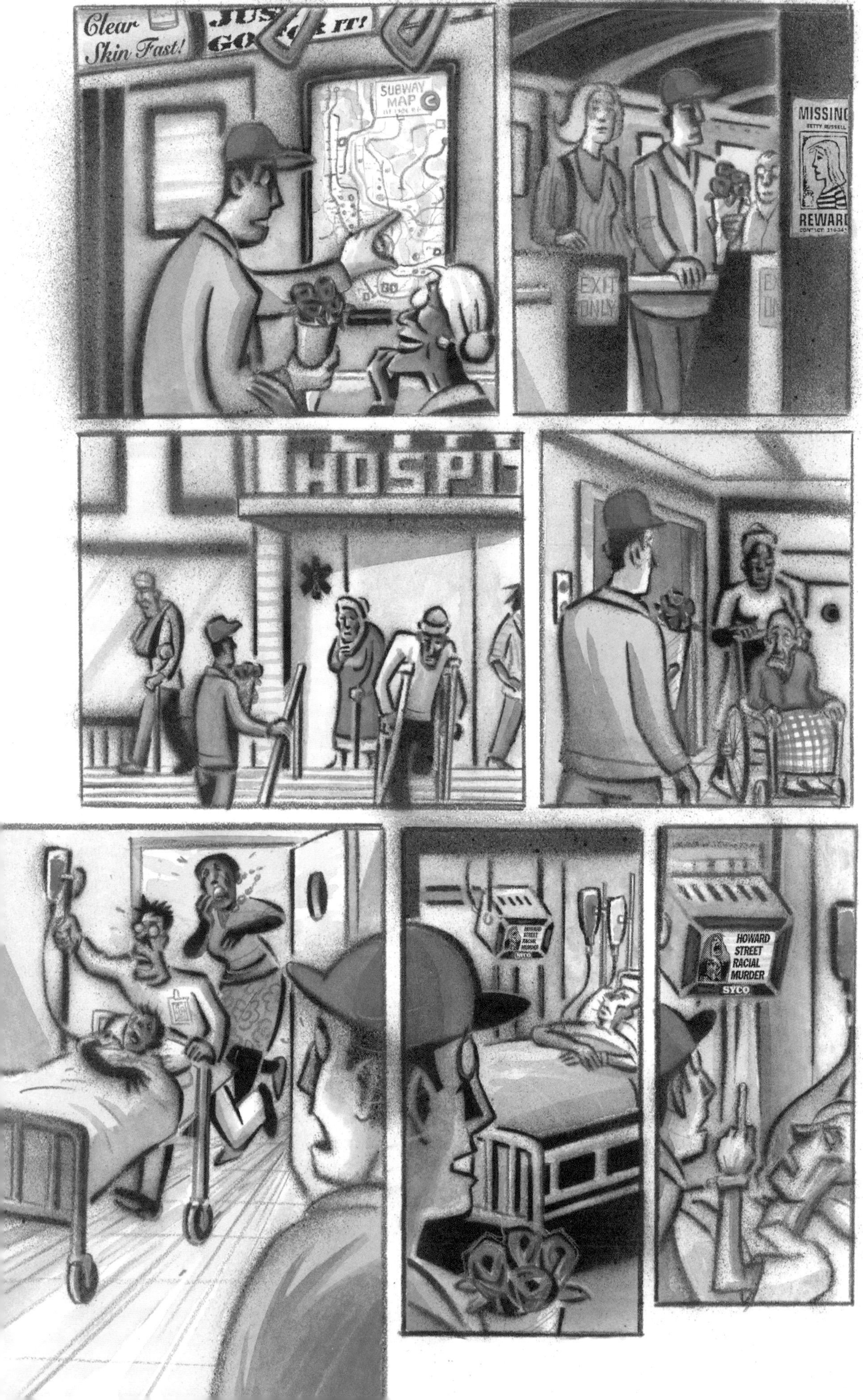
Clear Skin Fast!
JUS
GO R IT!
SUBWAY MAP
MISSING
BETTY RUSSELL
REWARD
EXIT ONLY
HOSPI
HOWARD STREET RACIAL MURDER
SYCO

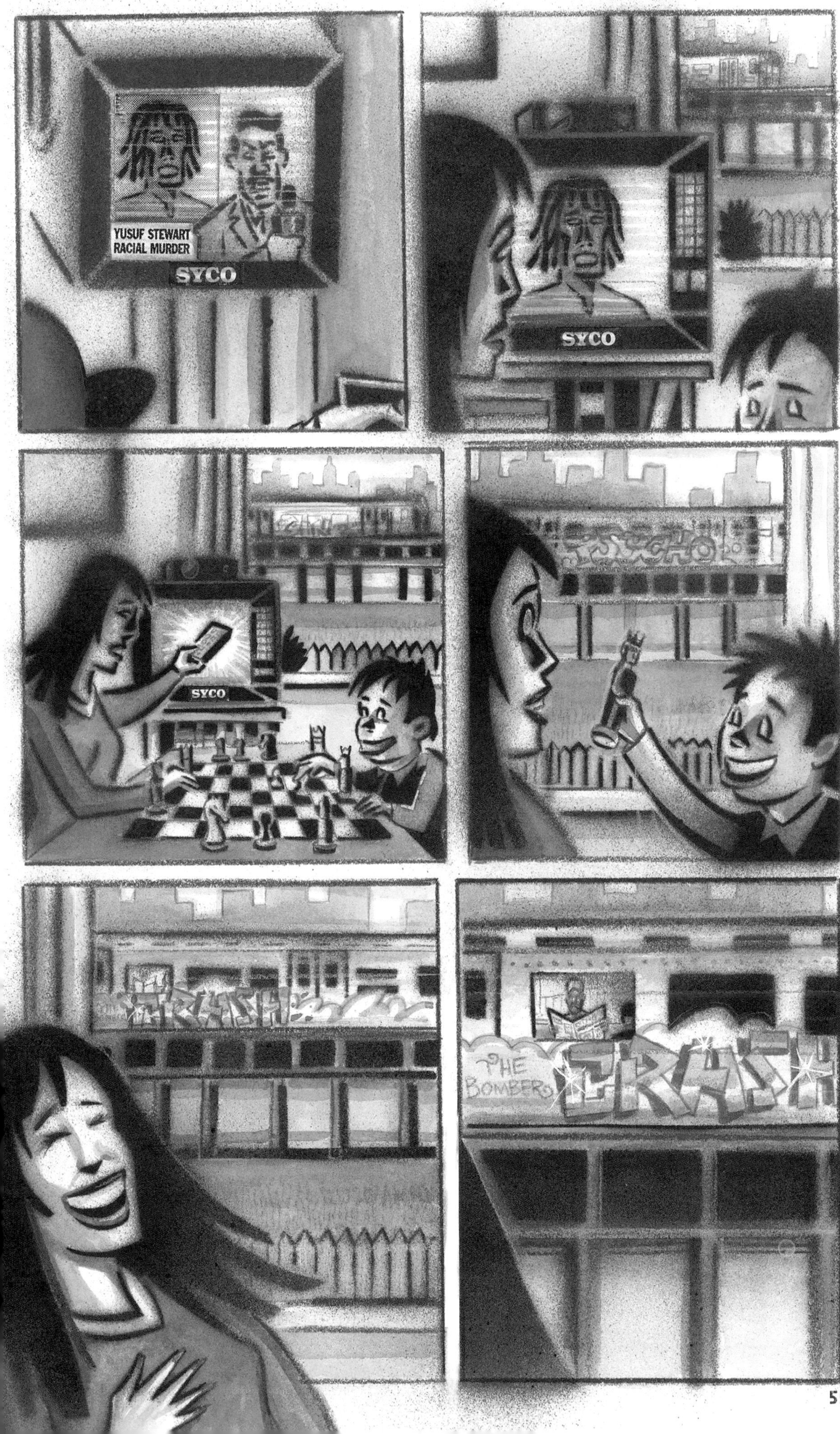
YUSUF STEWART
RACIAL MURDER
SYCO
SYCO
SYCO
THE BOMBERS

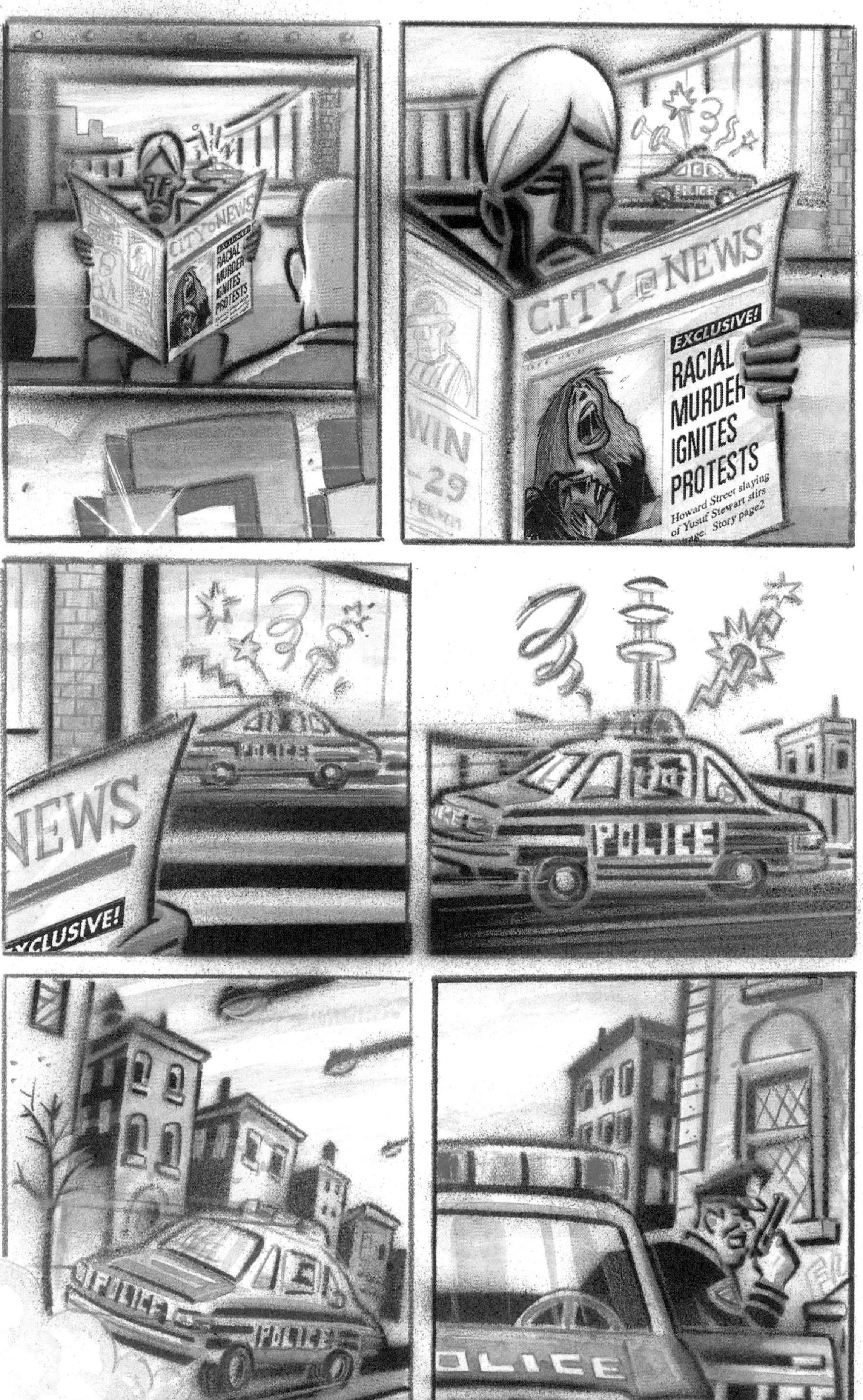
CITY NEWS
EXCLUSIVE!
RACIAL MURDER IGNITES PROTESTS
Howard Street slaying
of Yusuf Stewart stirs
Story page2
WIN
29
NEWS
EXCLUSIVE!
POLICE
POLICE
POLICE
POLICE
OLICE
ICE

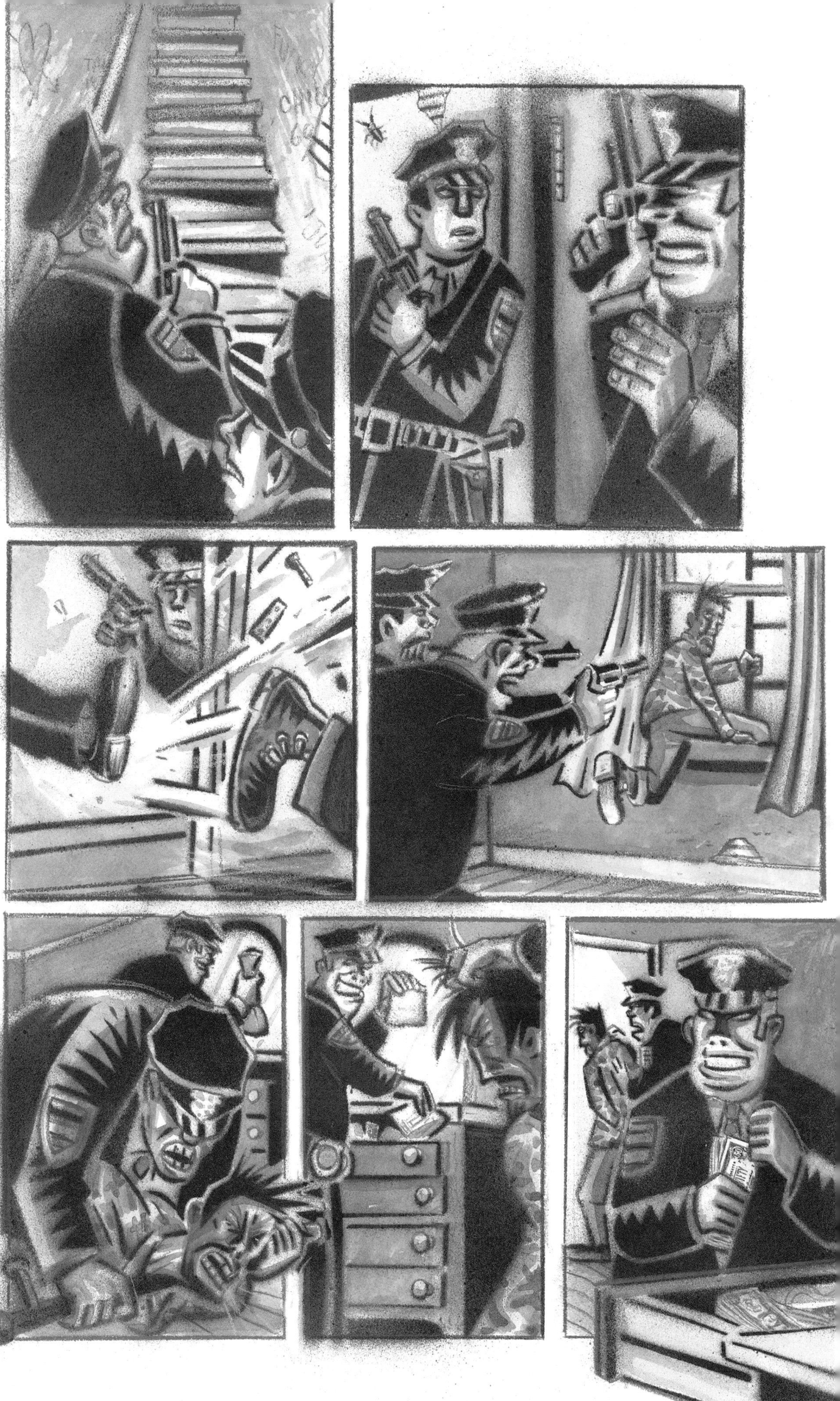

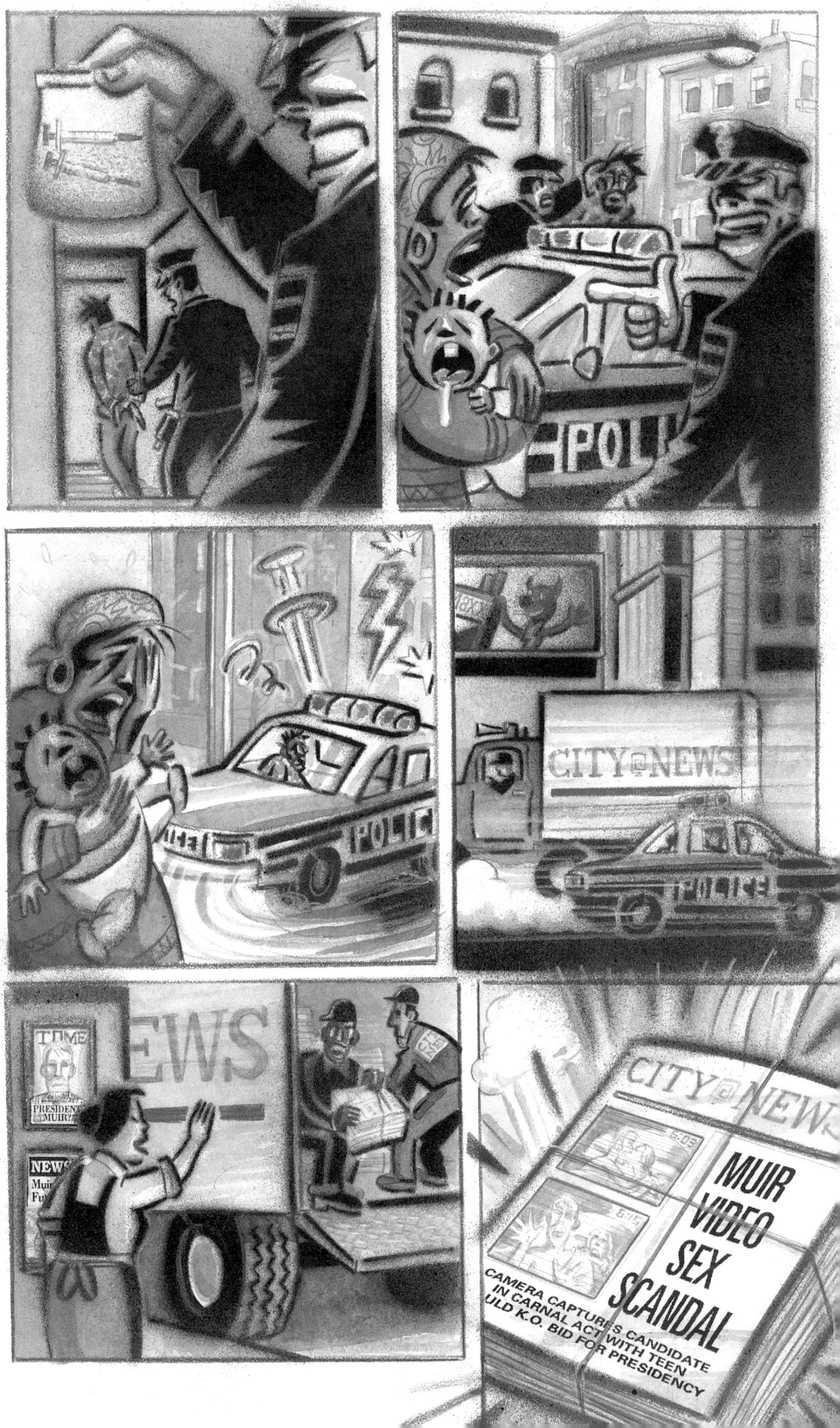
POLI
POLICE
CITY NEWS
POLICE
EWS
TIME
PRESIDENT MUIR?
NEWS
CITY NEWS
MUIR
VIDEO
SEX
SCANDAL
CAMERA CAPTURES CANDIDATE
IN CARNAL ACT WITH TEEN
ULD K.O. BID FOR PRESIDENCY

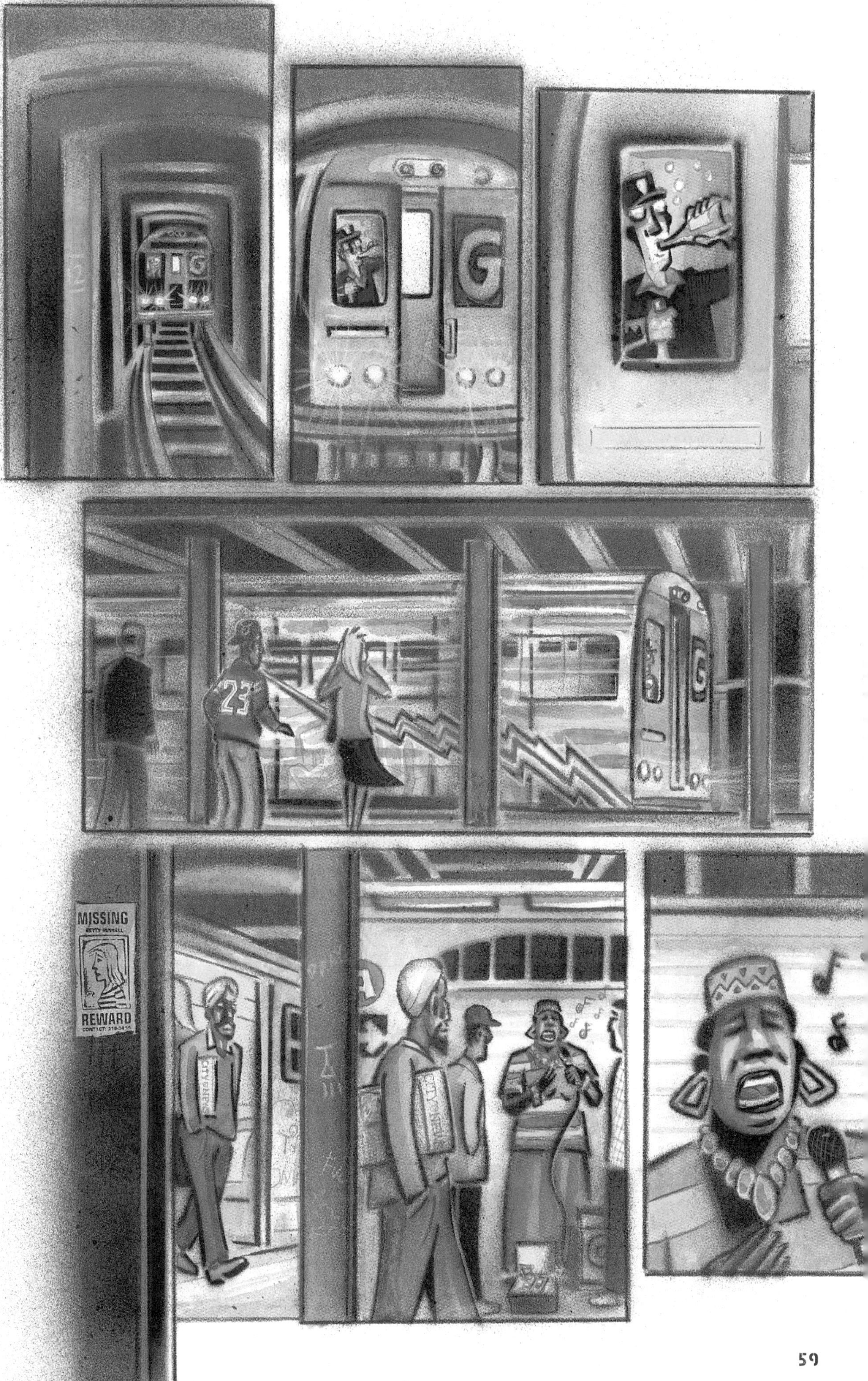
G
G
23
G
MISSING
REWARD

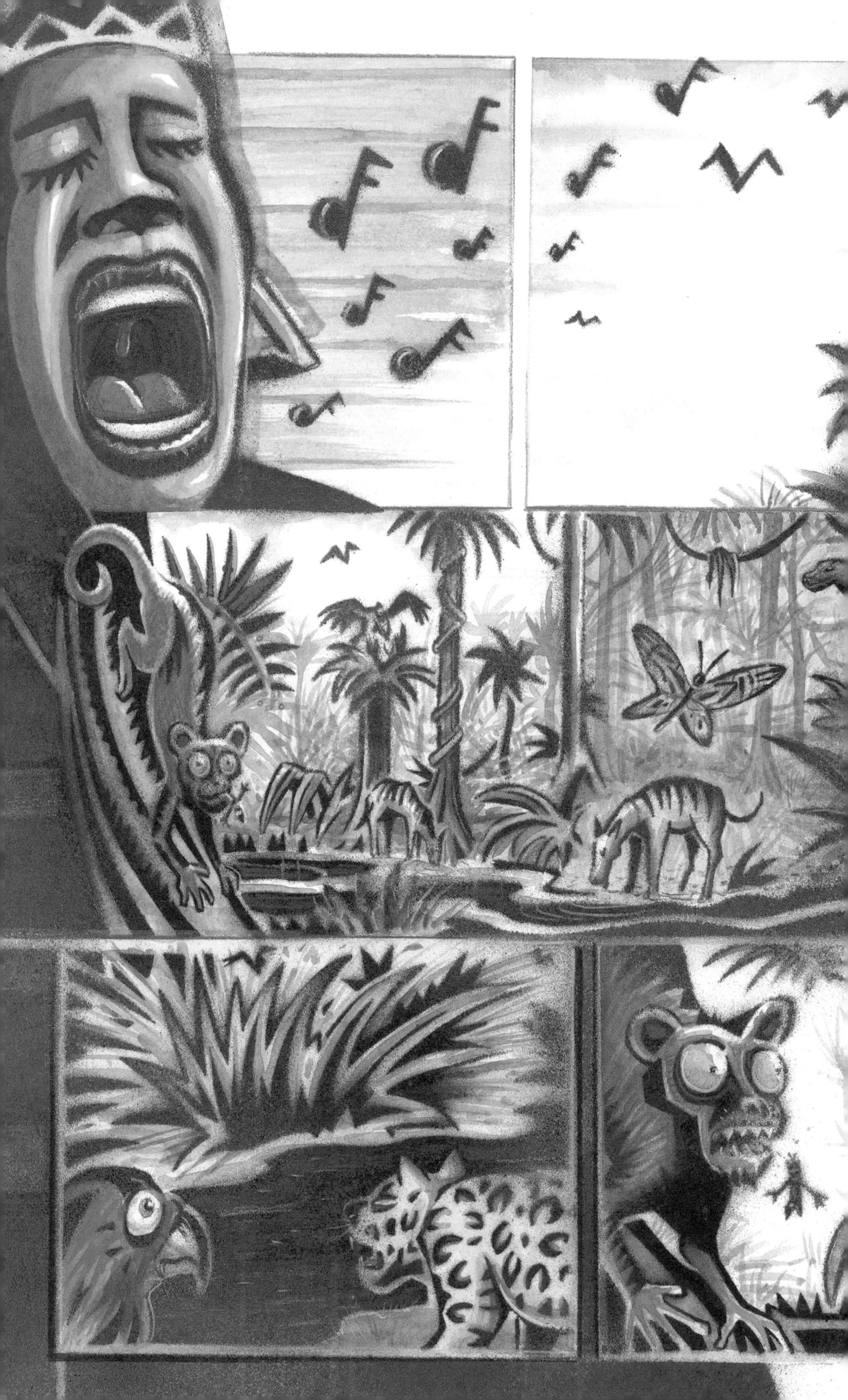

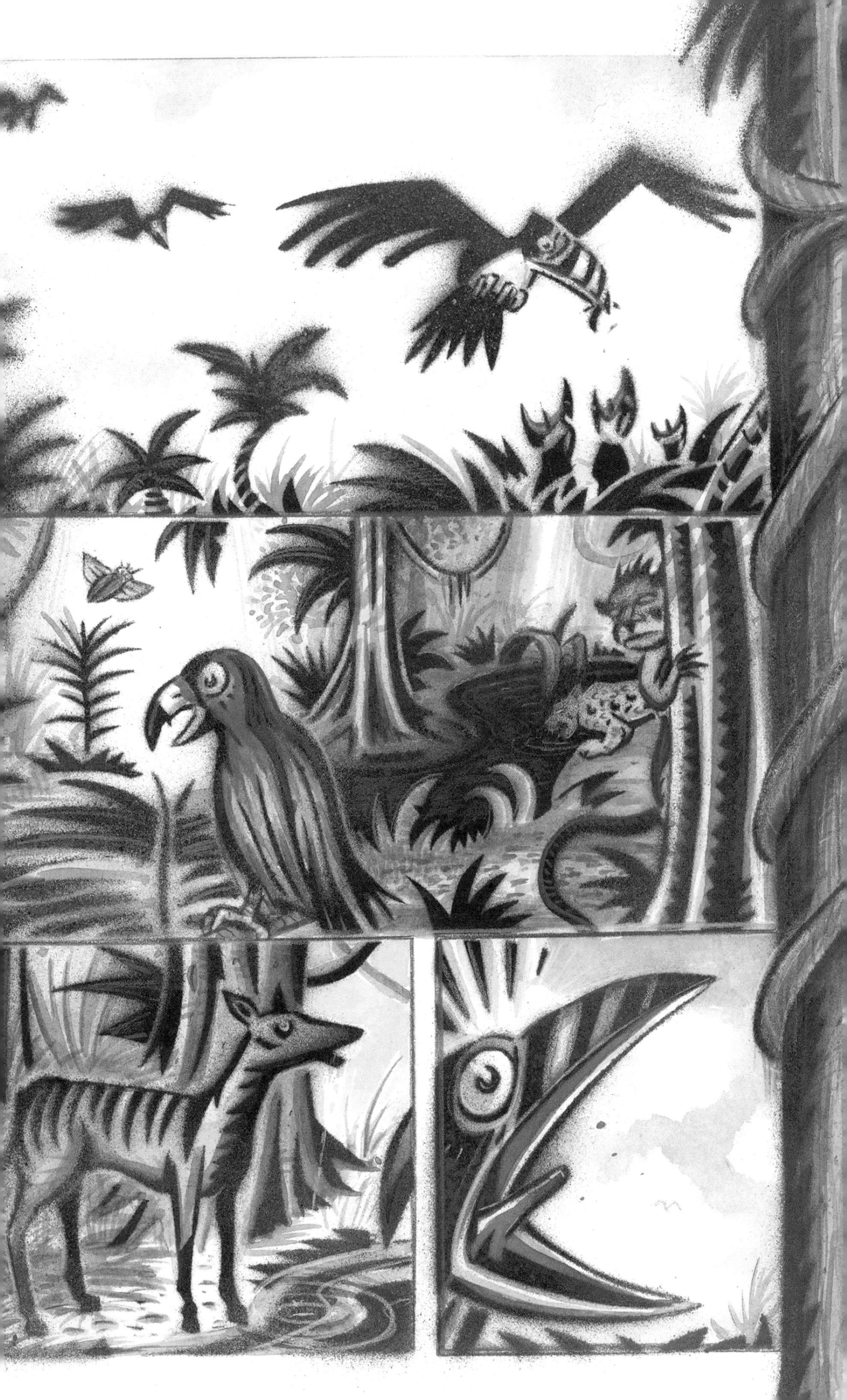

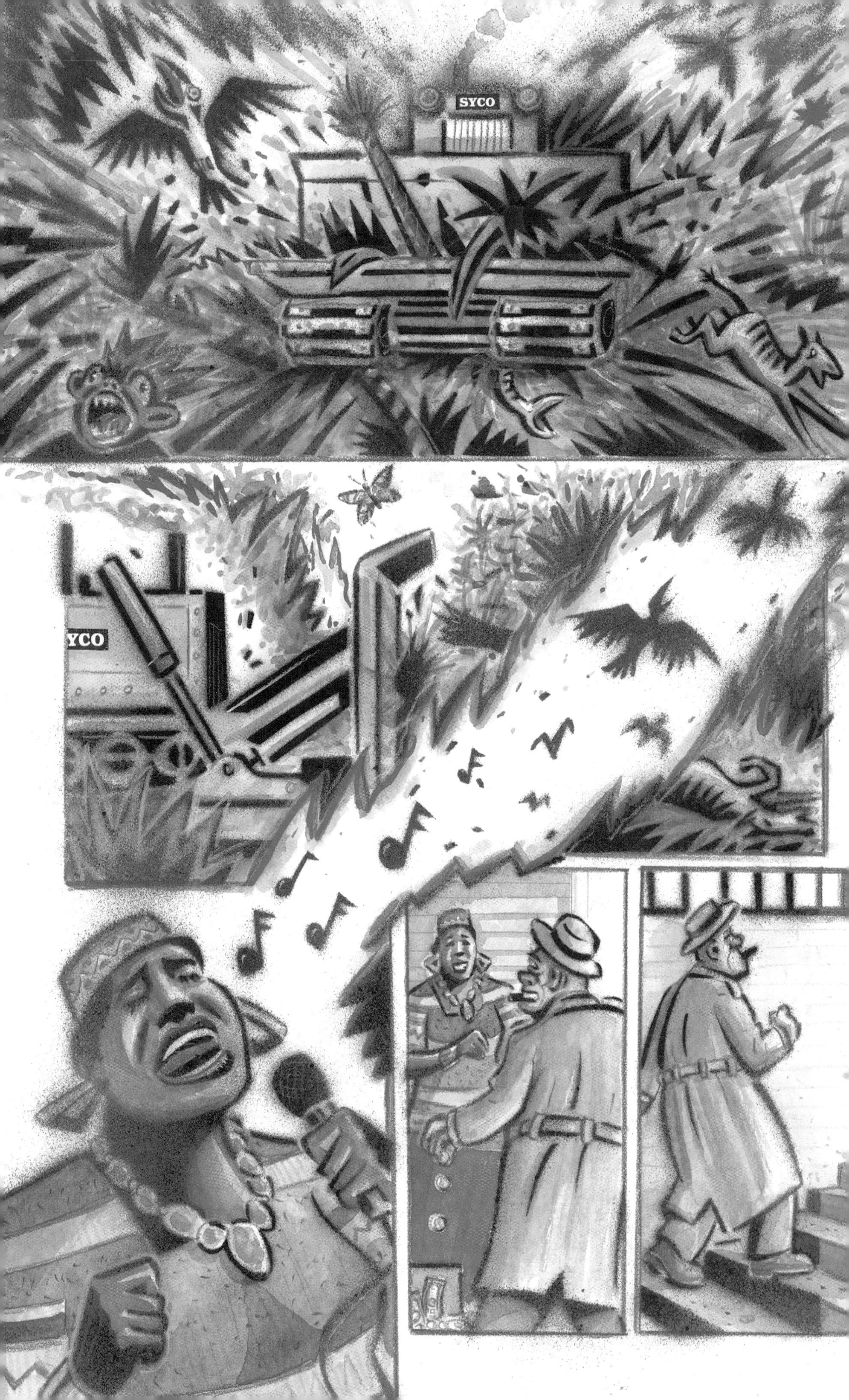
SYCO
YCO

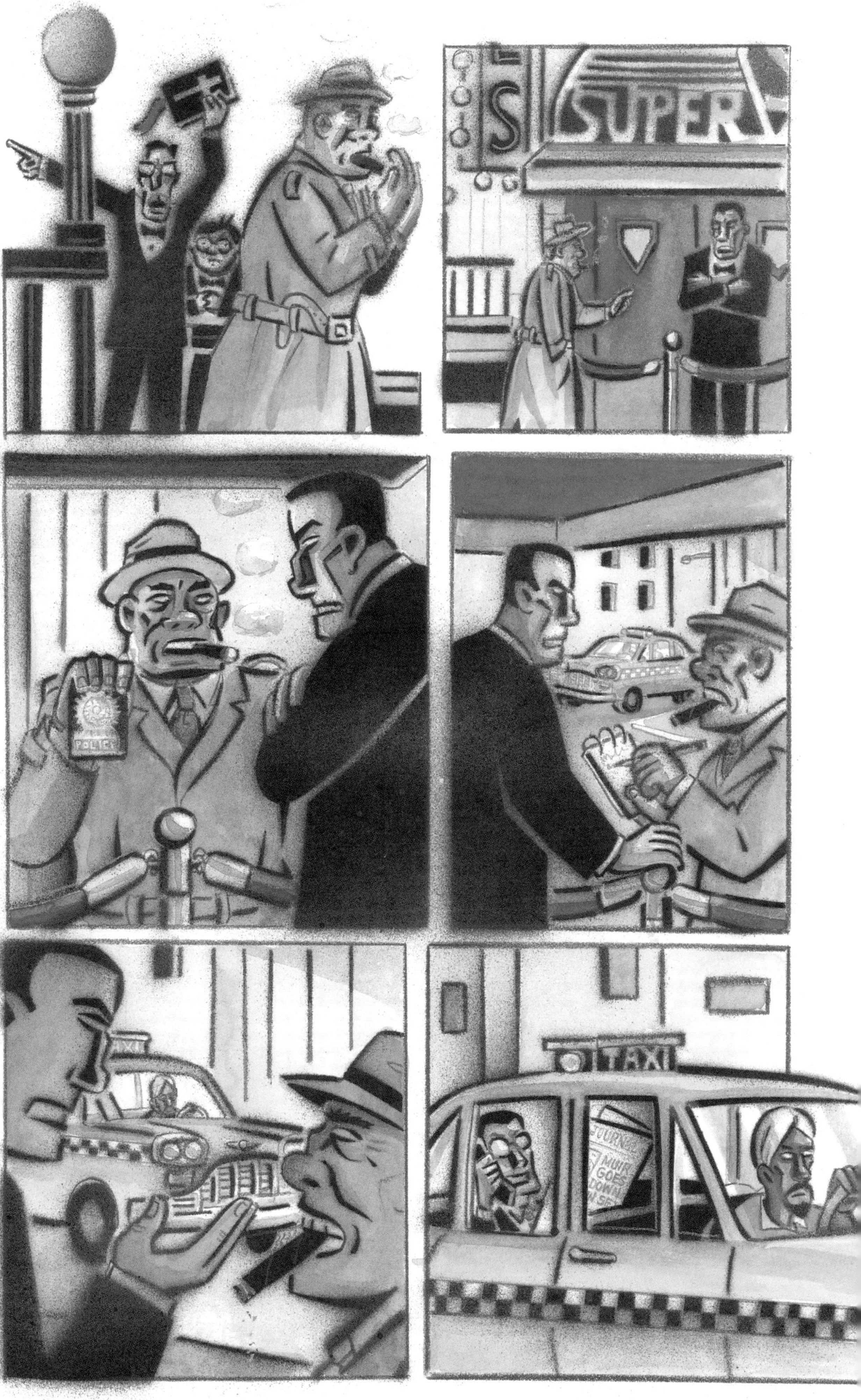
SUPER
POLICE
TAXI
GOES

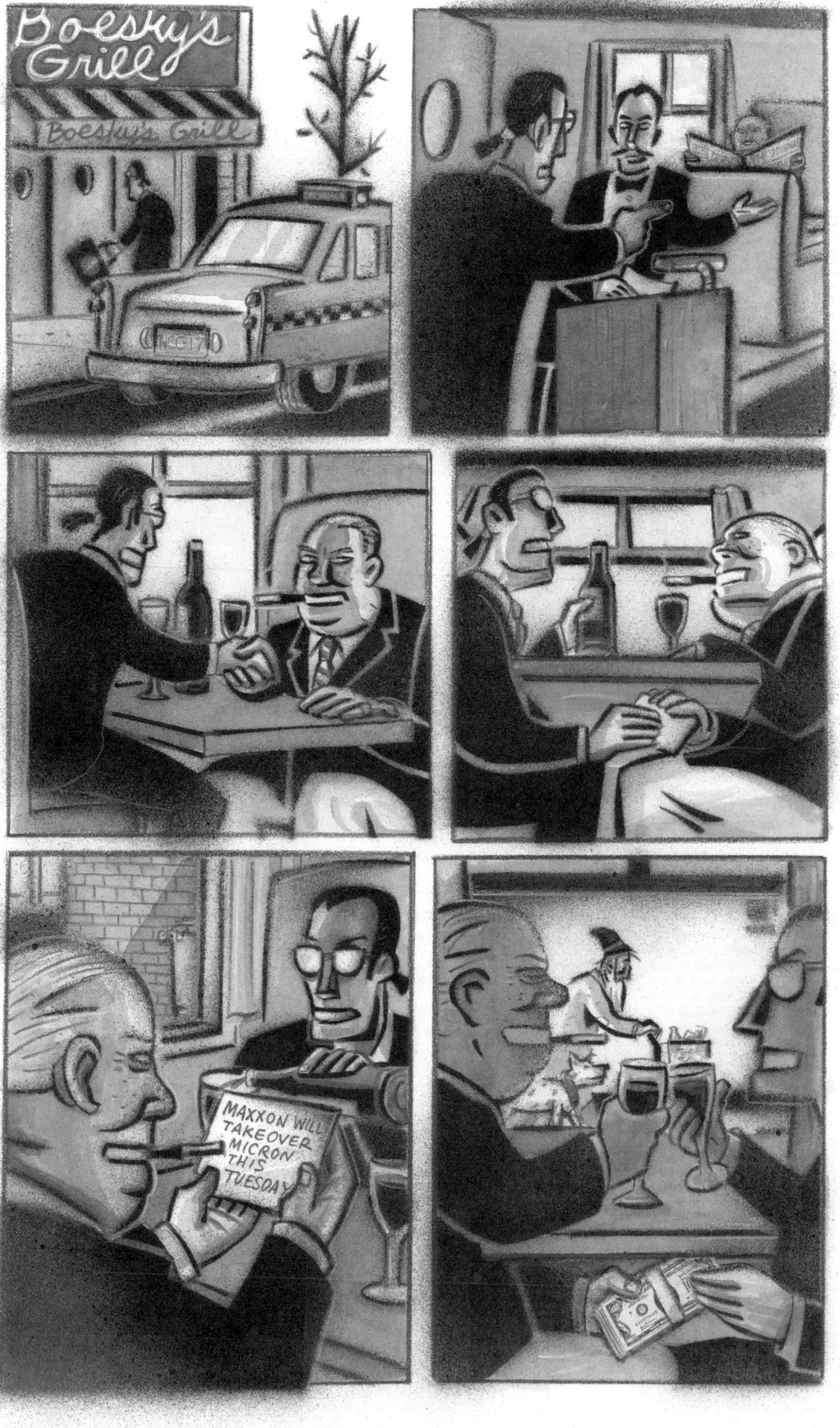
Boesky's Grill
Boesky's Grill
MAXXON WILL TAKEOVER MICRON THIS TUESDAY

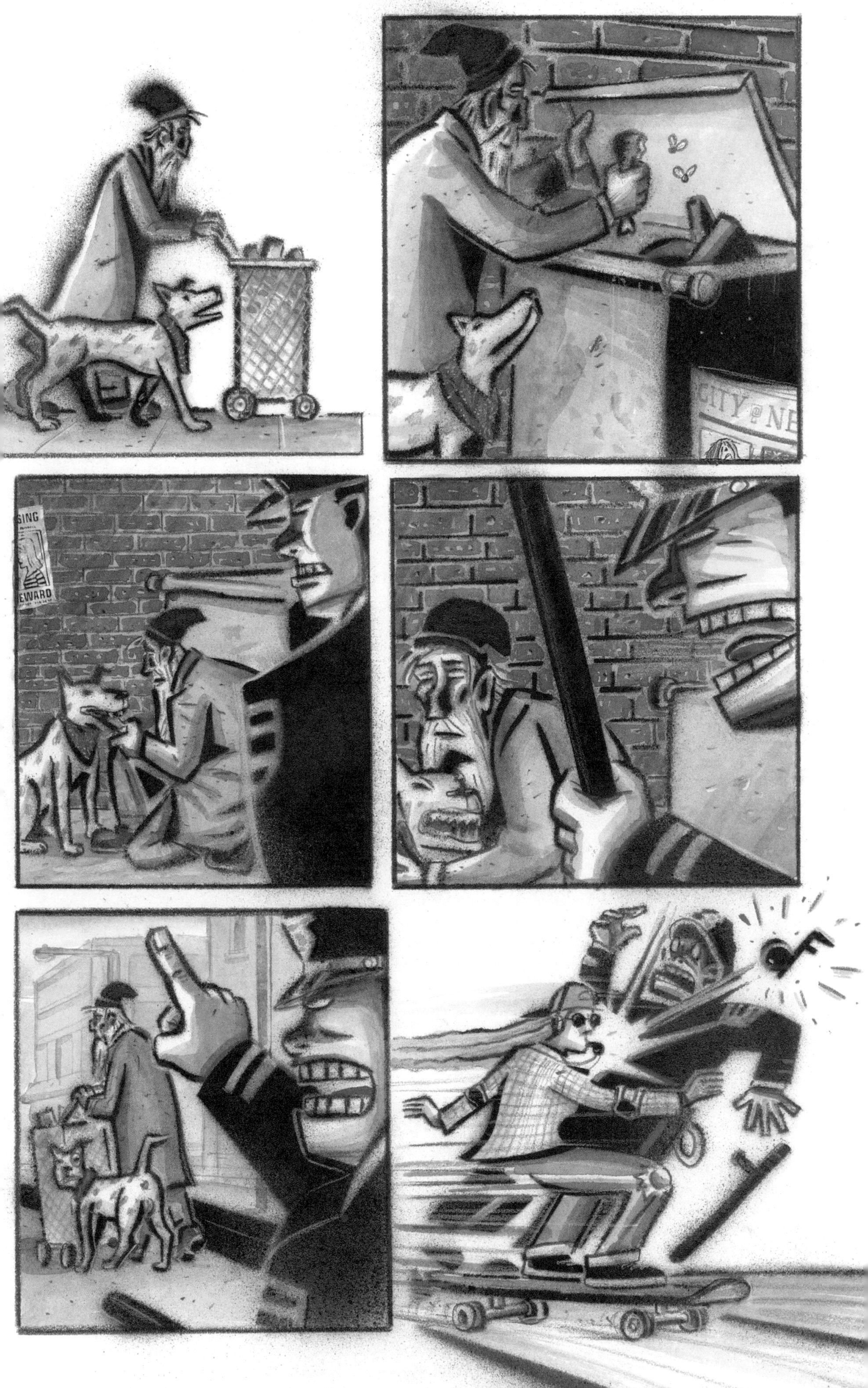
CITY NE
SING
EWARD

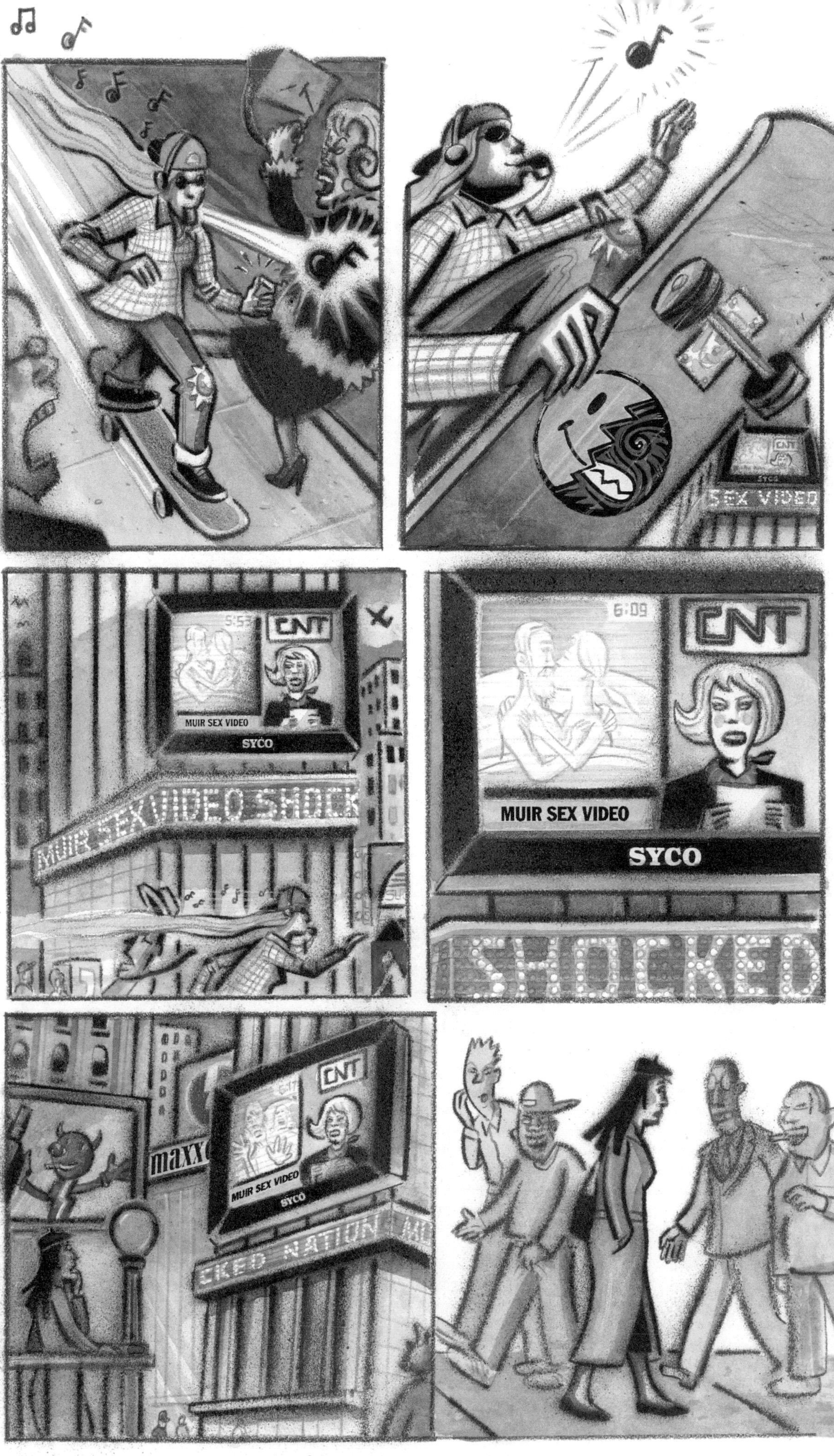
SEX VIDEO
CNT
SYCO
MUIR SEX VIDEO
MUIR SEX VIDEO SHOCK
6:09
CNT
MUIR SEX VIDEO
SYCO
SHOCKED
maxxe
CNT
MUIR SEX VIDEO
SYCO
CKED NATION

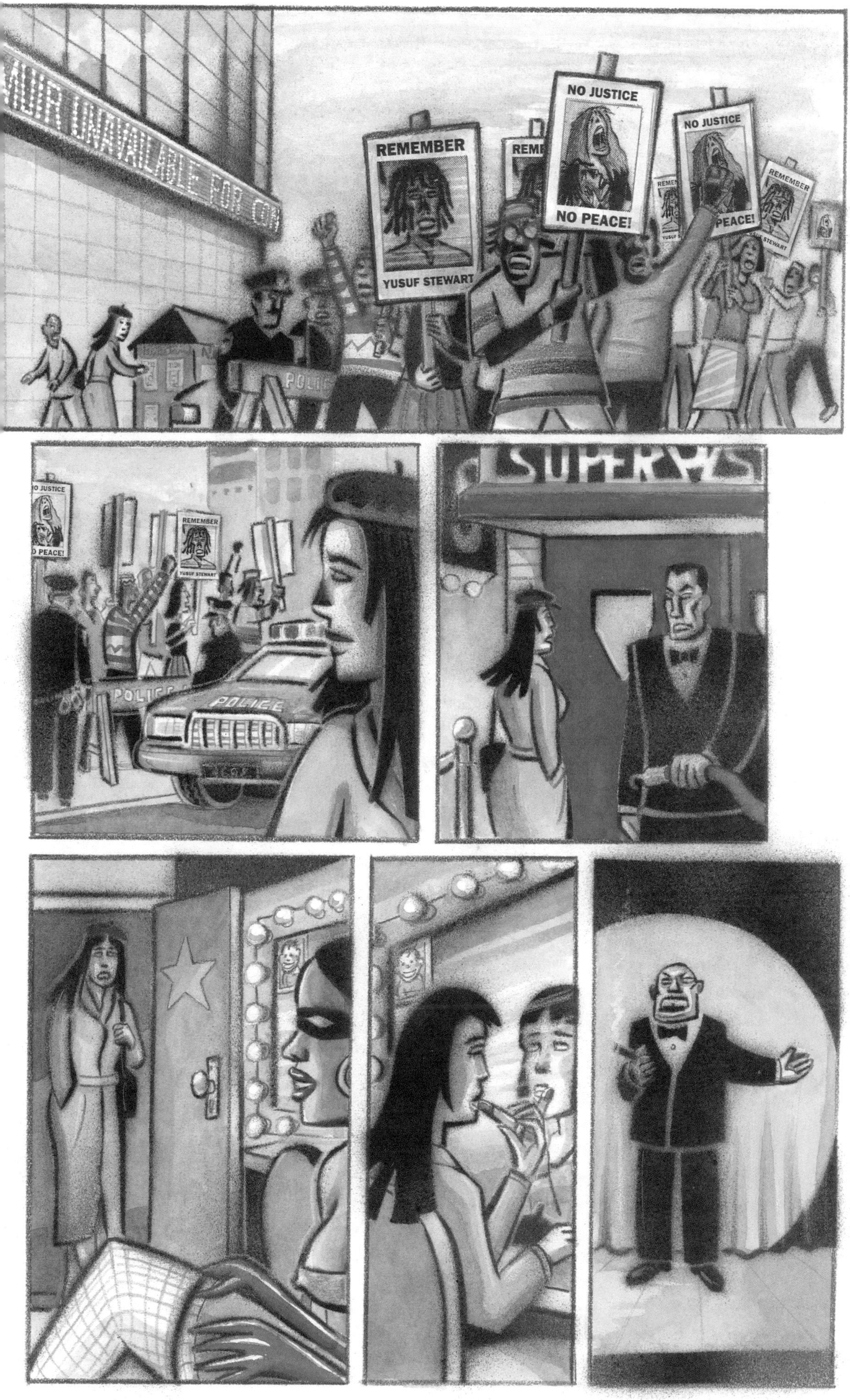
REMEMBER
YUSUF STEWART
NO JUSTICE
NO PEACE!
POLICE

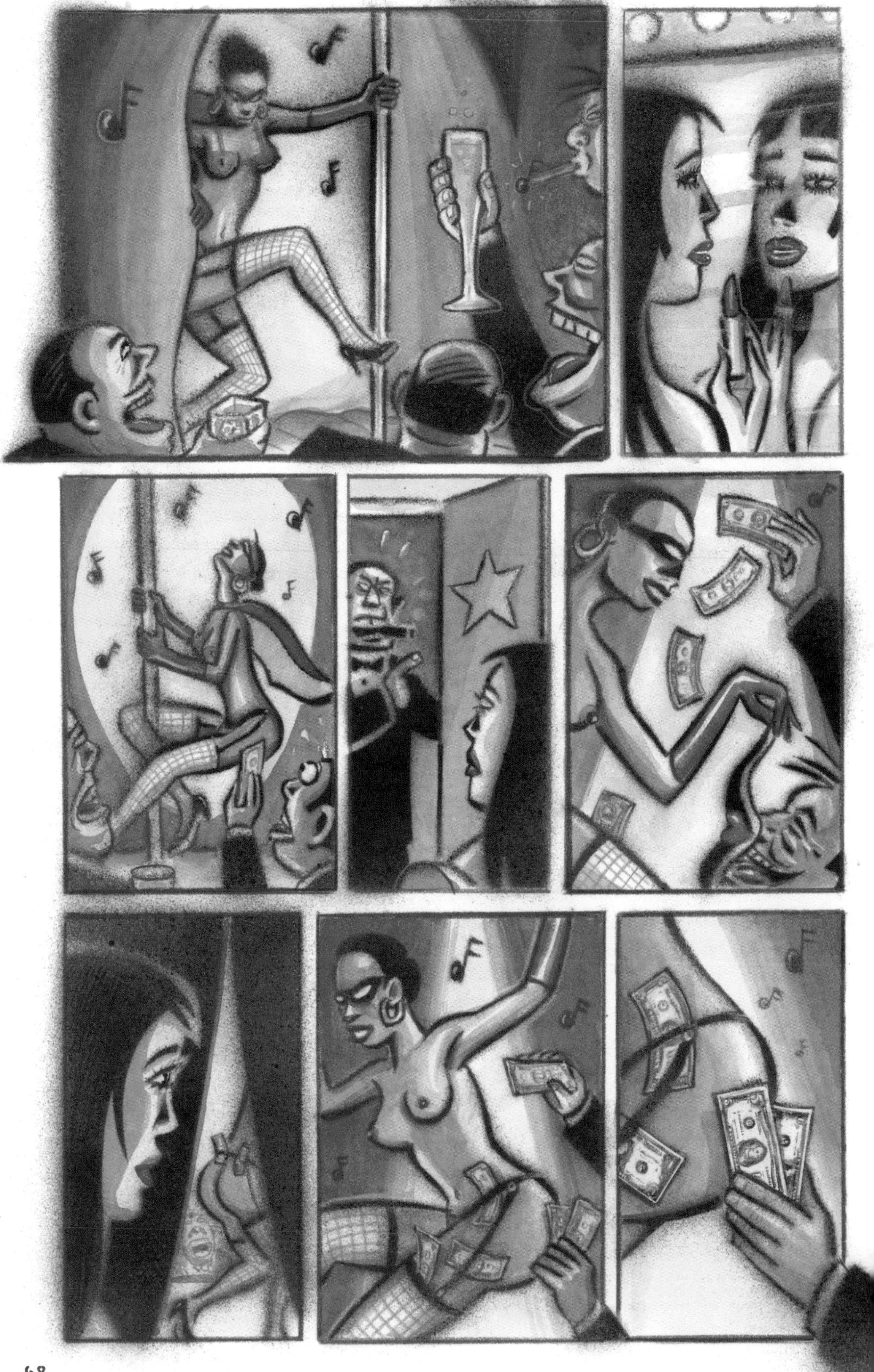

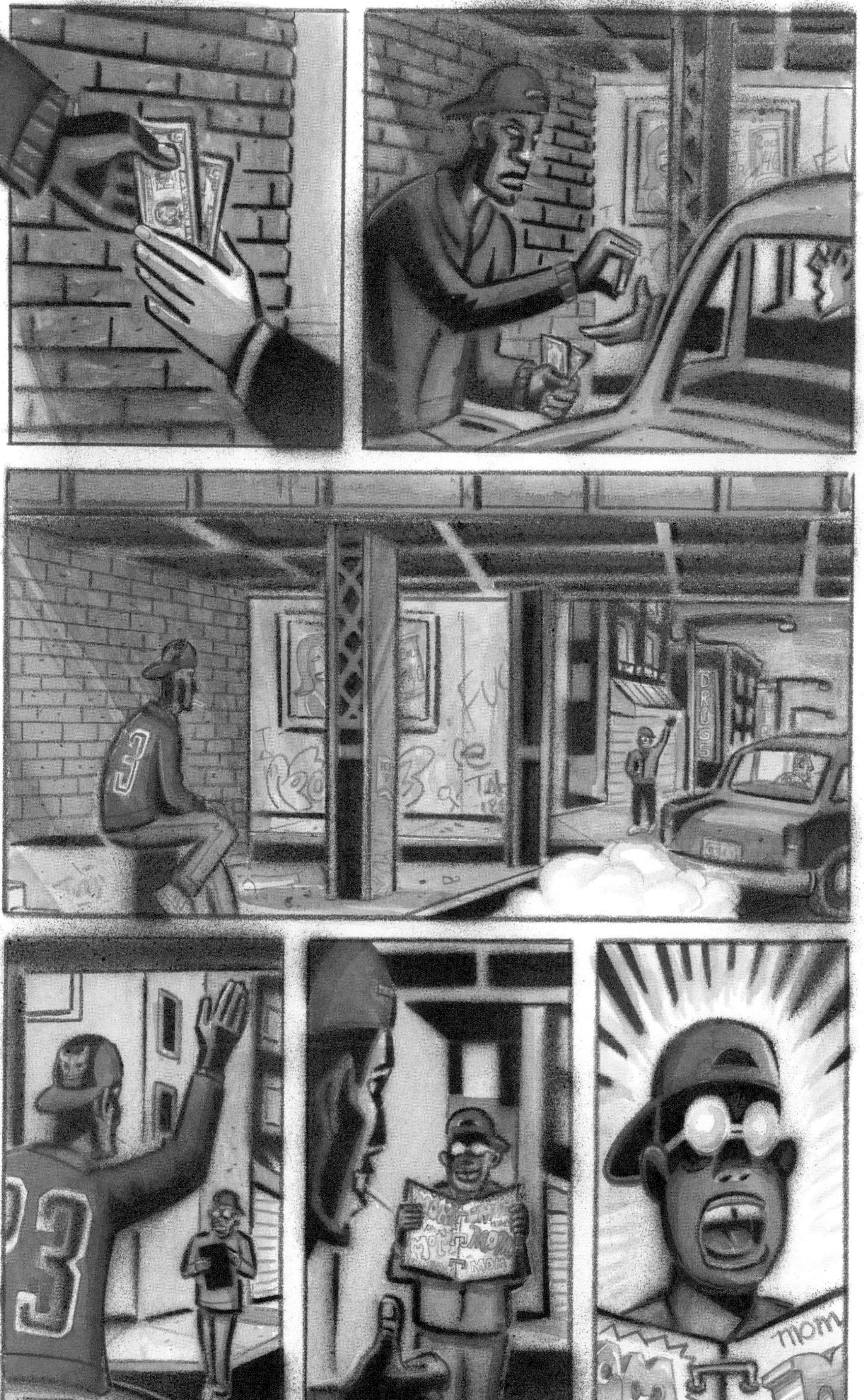
DRUGS
mom

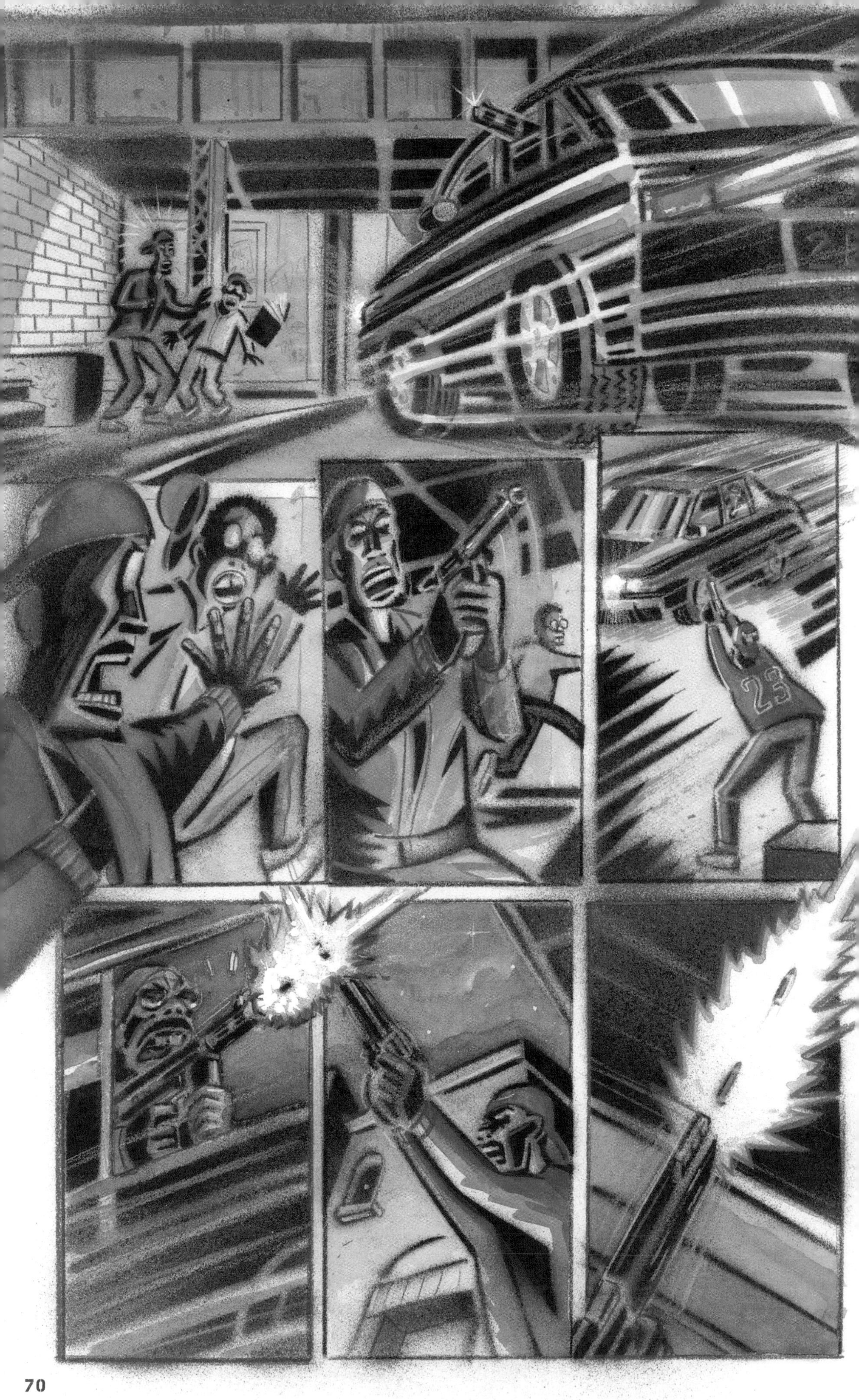

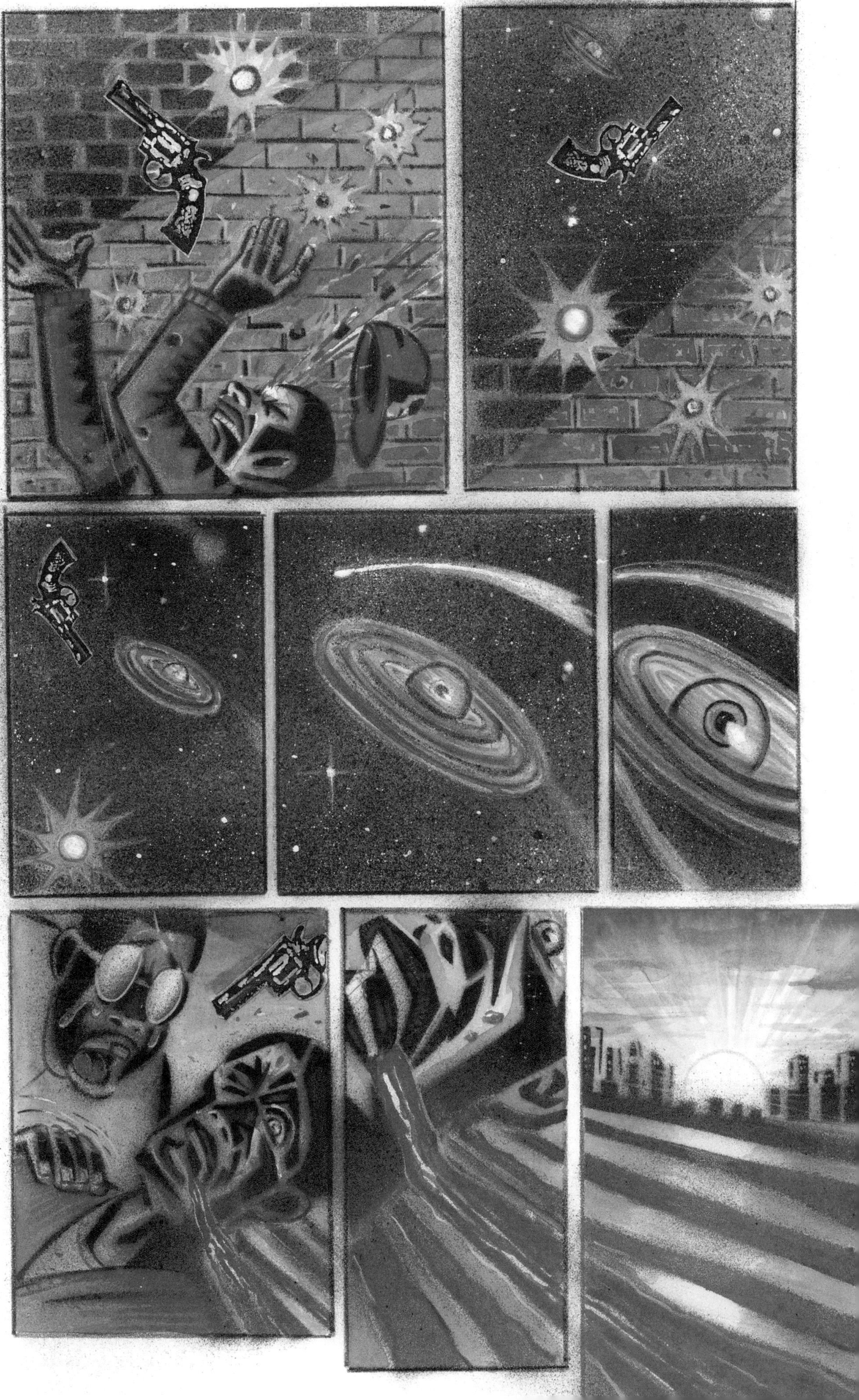

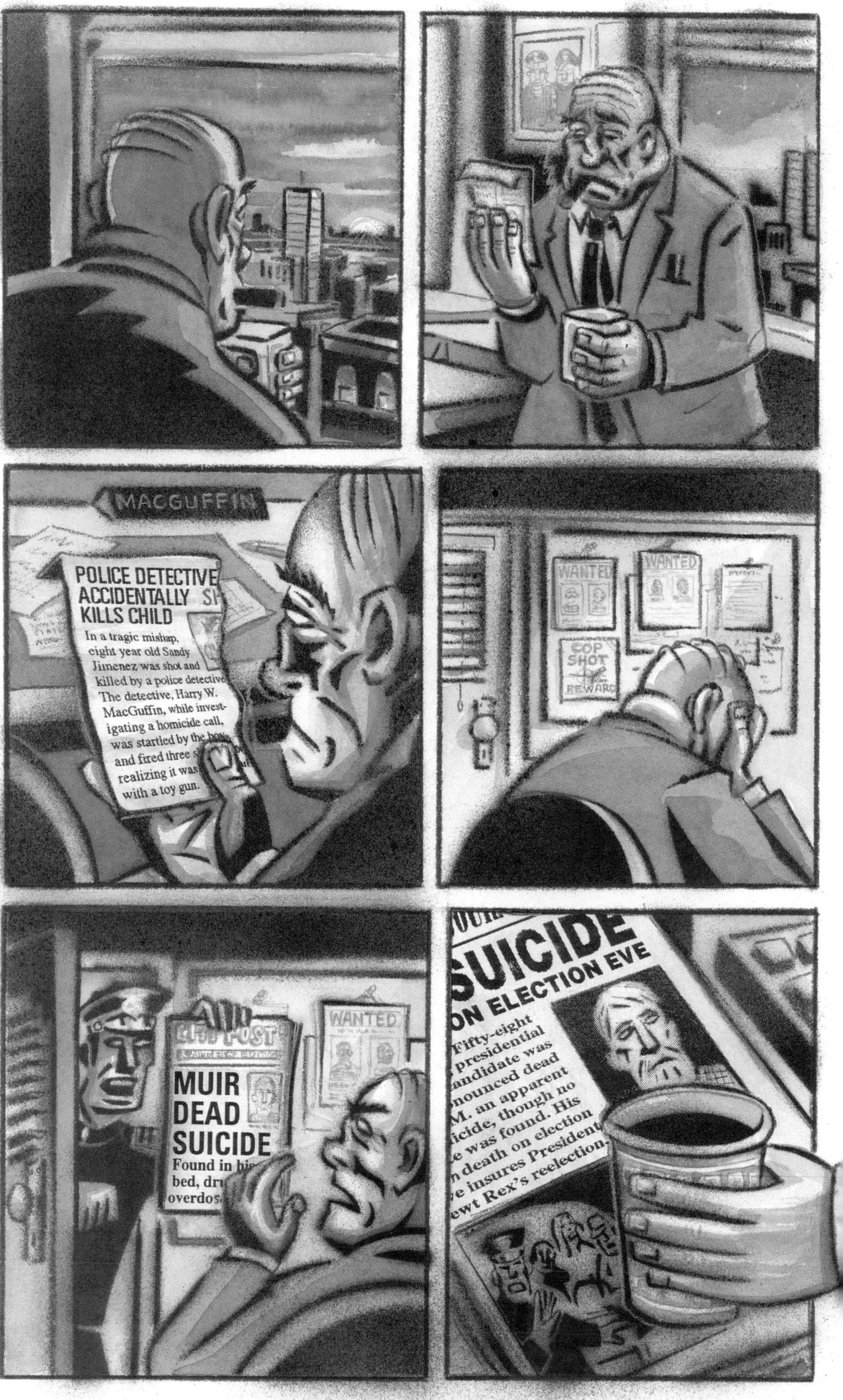
MACGUFFIN
POLICE DETECTIVE ACCIDENTALLY KILLS CHILD
In a tragic mishap, eight year old Sandy Jimenez was shot and killed by a police detective. The detective, Harry W. MacGuffin, while investigating a homicide call, was startled by the
and fired three
realizing it was
with a toy gun.
WANTED
WANTED
COP SHOT
REWARD
MUIR DEAD SUICIDE
Found in
bed, dr
overdos
WANTED
SUICIDE
ON ELECTION EVE
Fifty-eight
presidential
andidate was
nounced dead
M. an apparent
icide, though no
was found. His
death on election
insures President
ewt Rex's reelection.

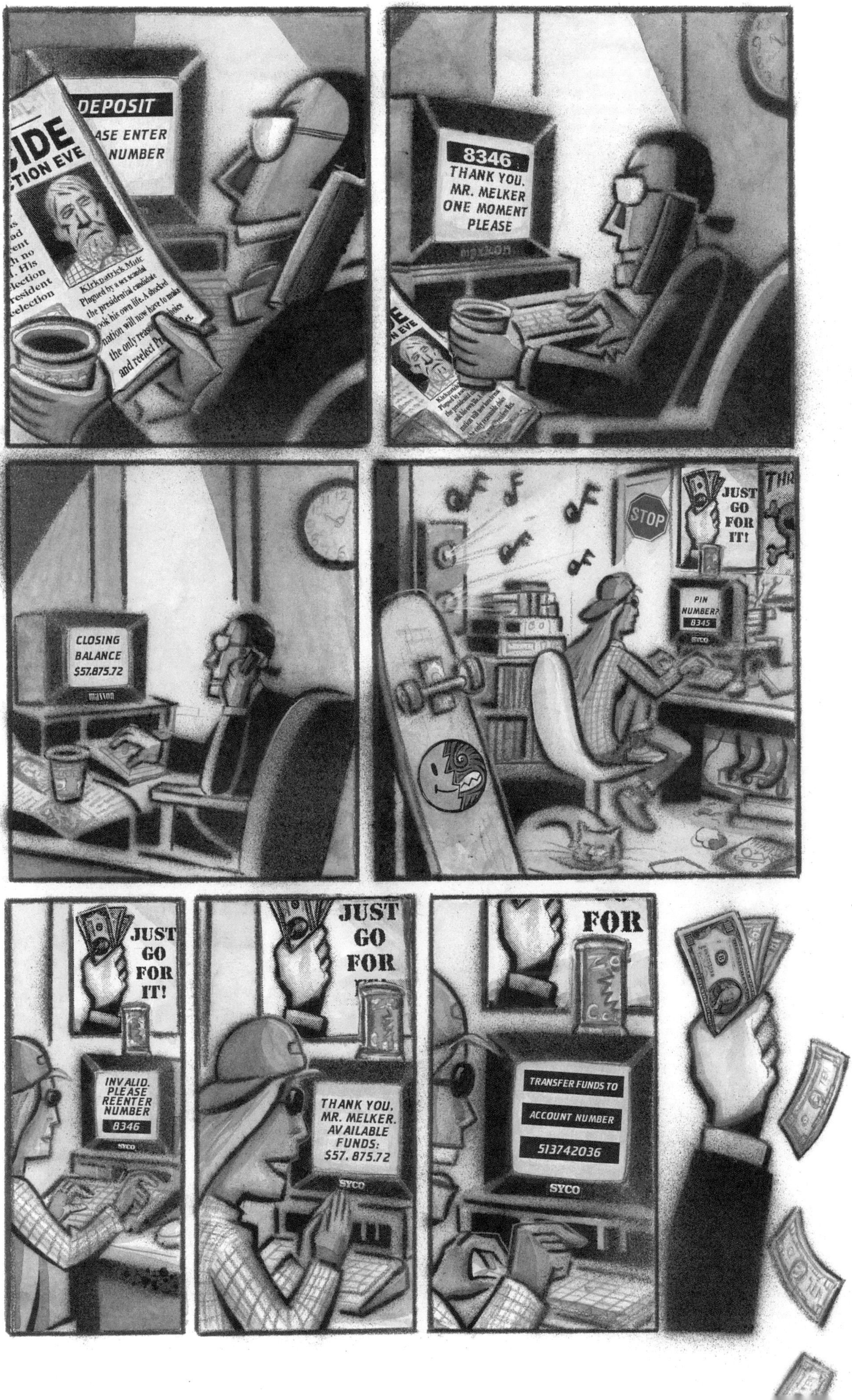

DEPOSIT
ASE ENTER
NUMBER
CIDE
CTION EVE
Plagued by a sex scandal
the presidential candidate
8346
THANK YOU.
MR. MELKER
ONE MOMENT
PLEASE
maxxon
CLOSING
BALANCE
$57.875.72
maxxon
STOP
JUST
GO
FOR
IT!
PIN
NUMBER?
8345
SYCO
JUST
GO
FOR
IT!
INVALID.
PLEASE
REENTER
NUMBER
8346
SYCO
JUST
GO
FOR
THANK YOU.
MR. MELKER.
AVAILABLE
FUNDS:
$57.875.72
SYCO
FOR
TRANSFER FUNDS TO
ACCOUNT NUMBER
513742036
SYCO

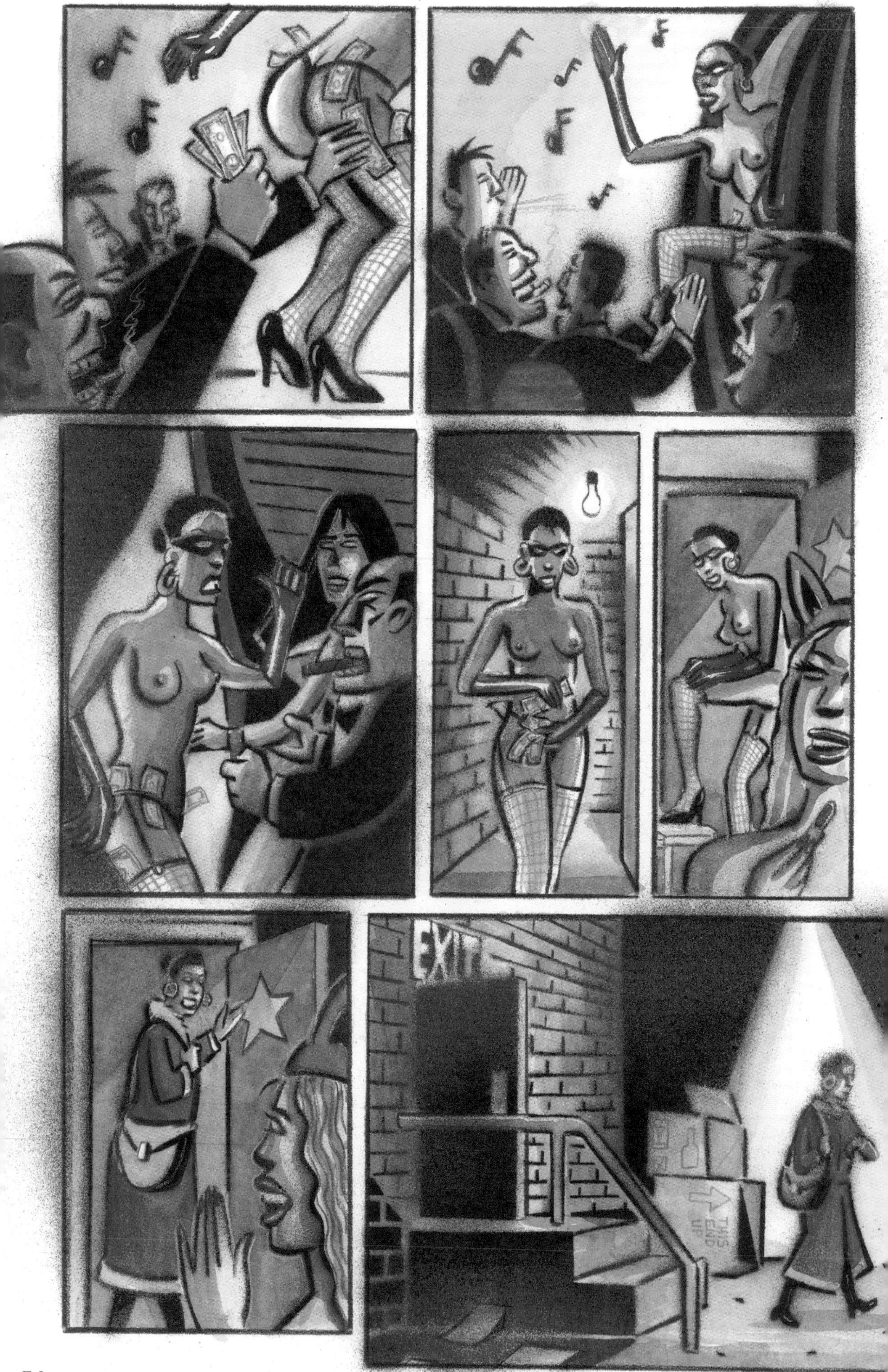
EXIT
THIS END UP

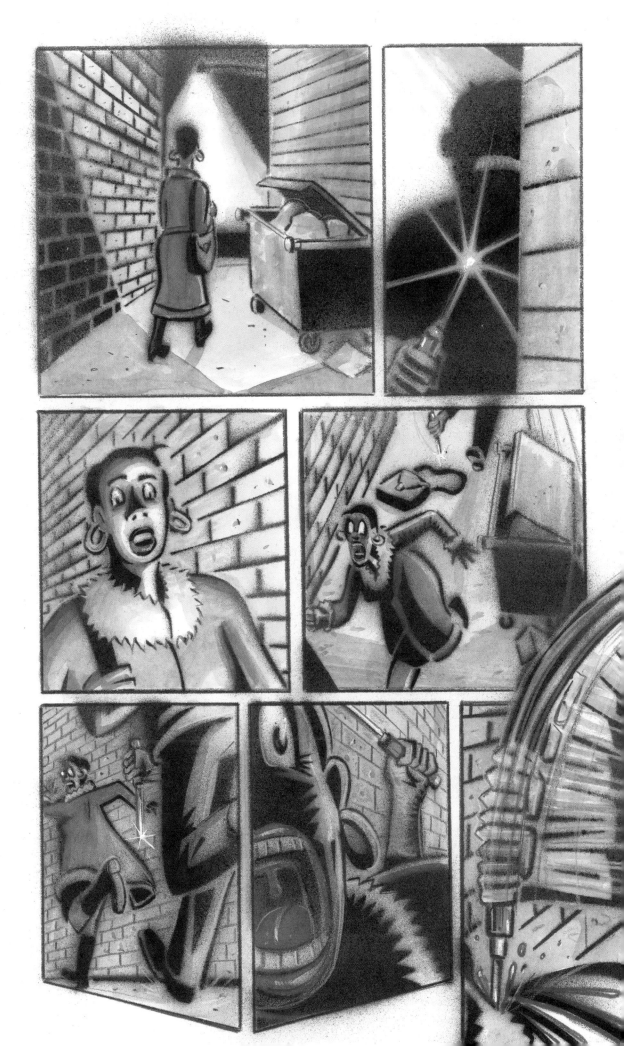

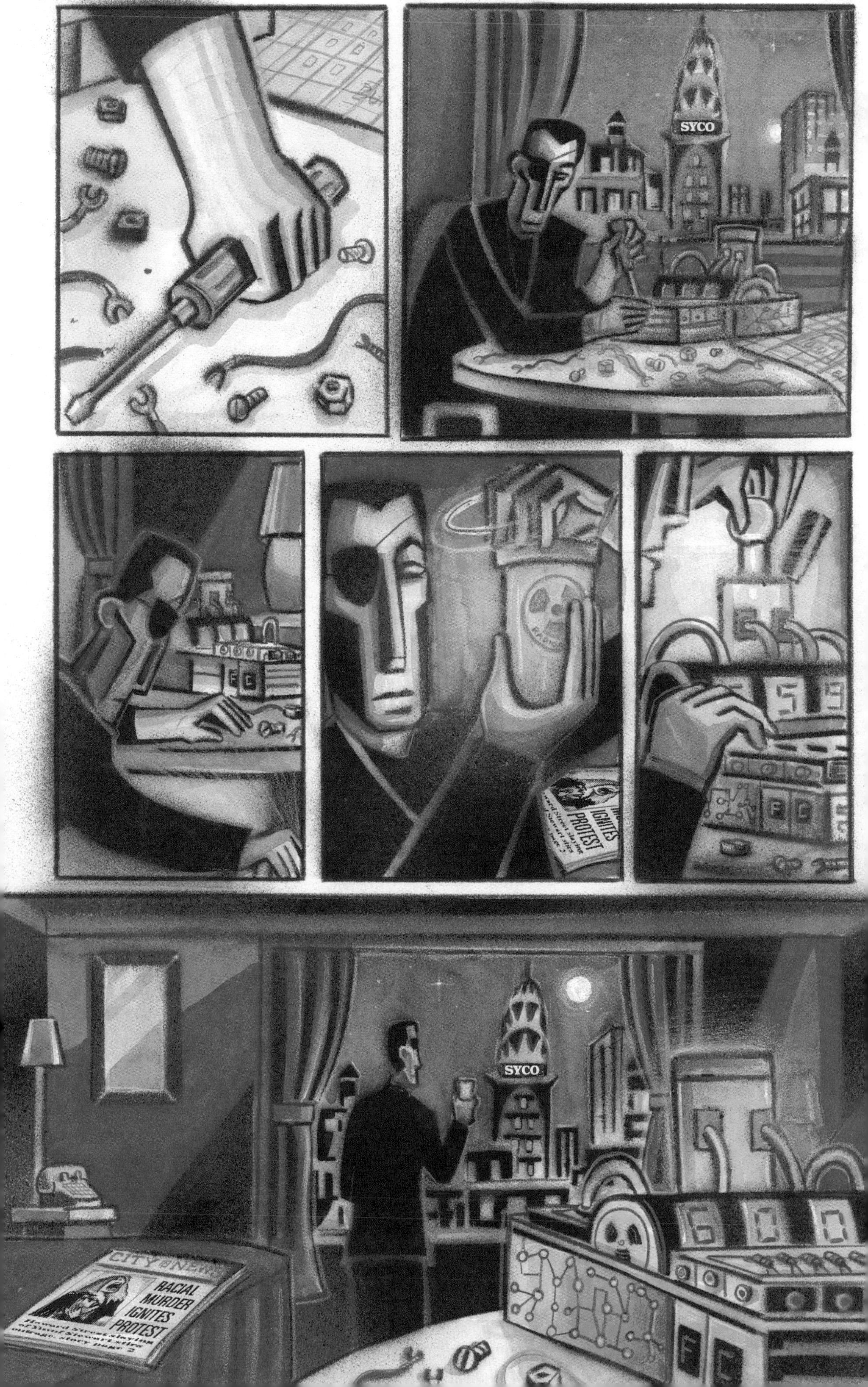
SYCO
IGNITES
PROTEST
SYCO
CITY NEWS
RACIAL
MURDER
IGNITES
PROTEST
Howard Street slaying
of Yusuf Stewart stirs
outrage. story page 2

"Star after star from Heaven's
high arch shall rush,
Suns sink on suns, and systems
systems crush,
Headlong, extinct, to one dark
centre fall,
And Death, and Night, and Chaos
mingle all!"

—ERASMUS DARWIN

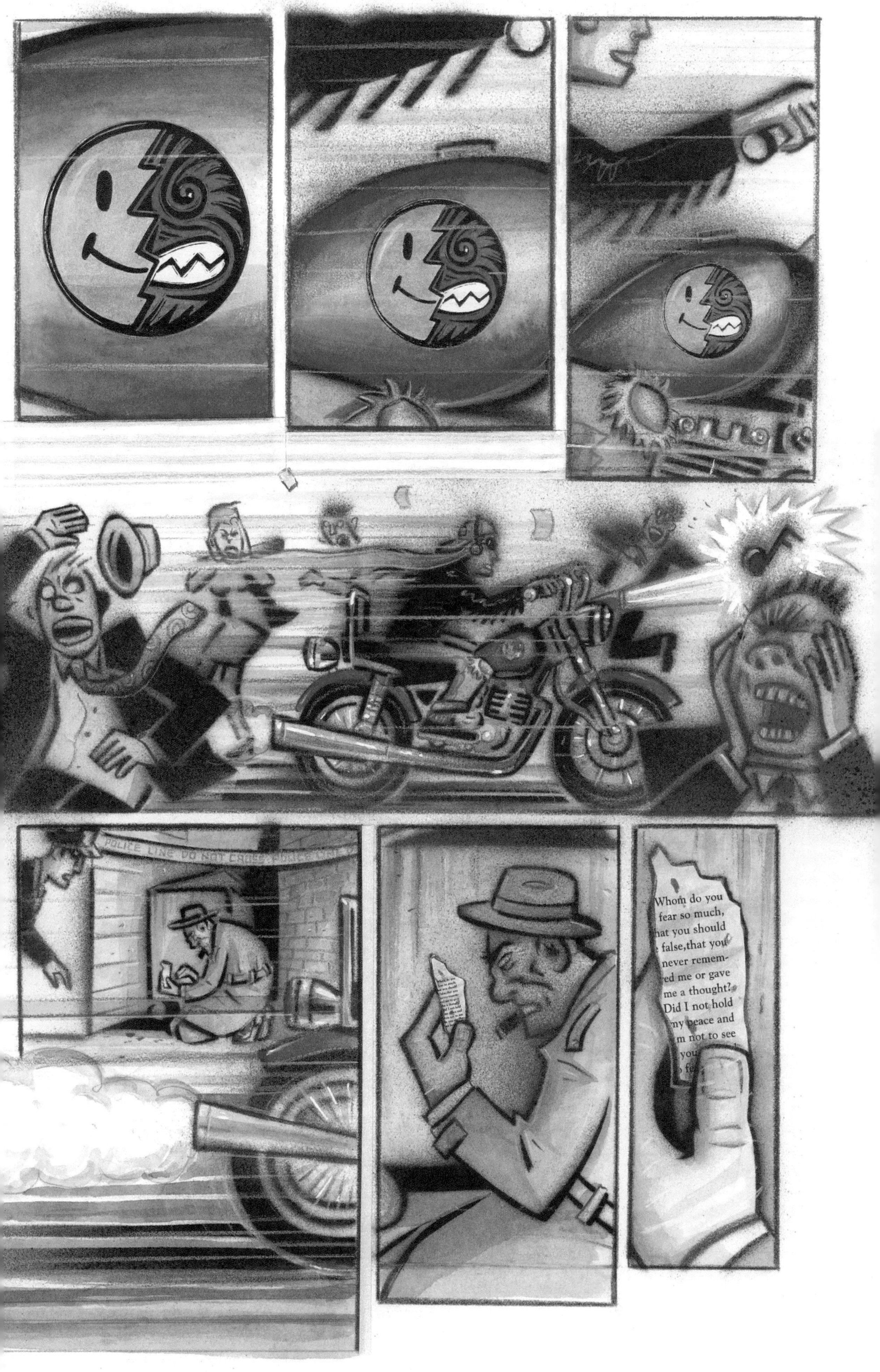
POLICE LINE DO NOT CROSS
Whom do you
fear so much,
hat you should
false,that you
never remem-
ed me or gave
me a thought?
Did I not hold
my peace and
m not to see
you

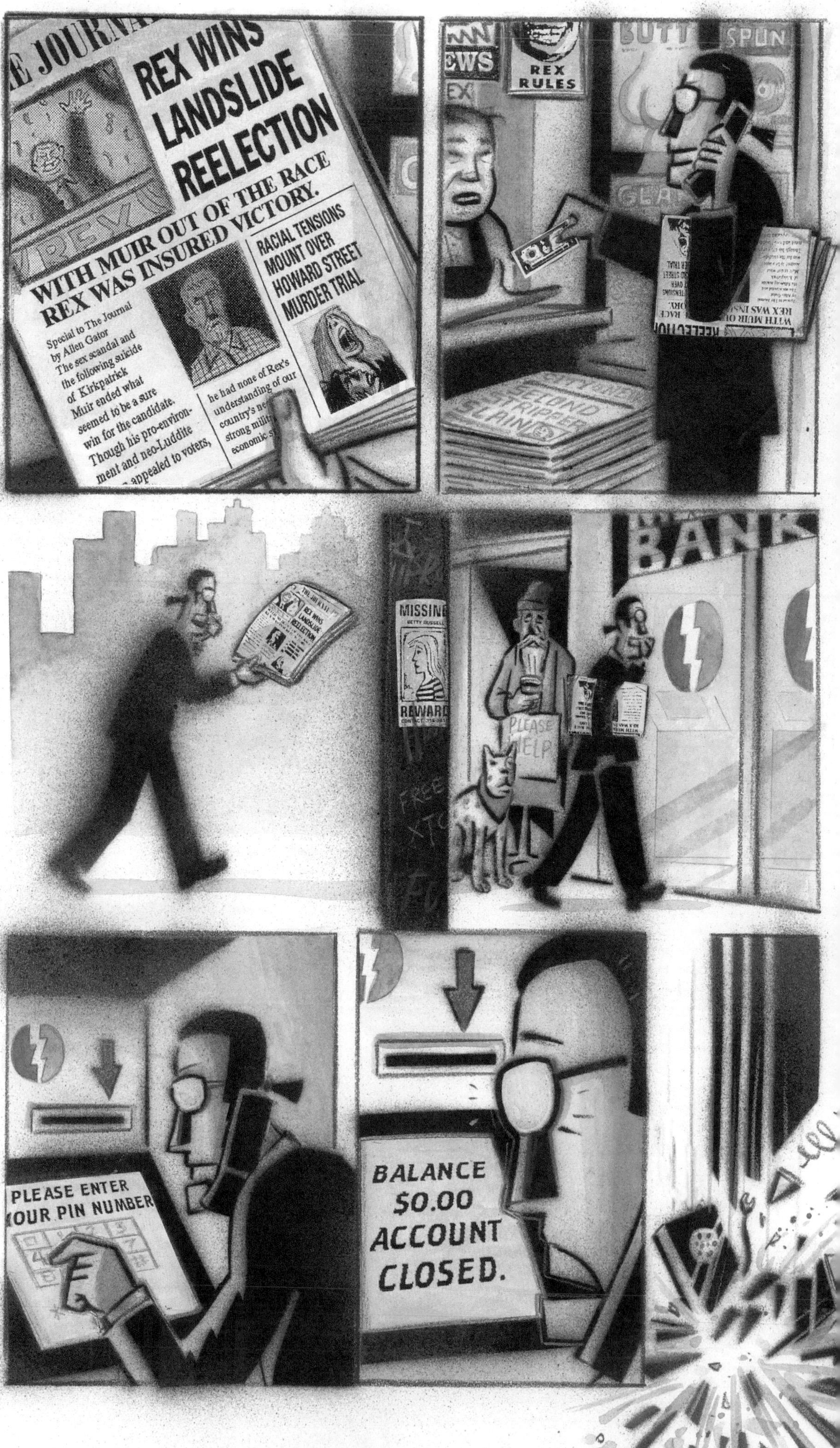
REX WINS LANDSLIDE REELECTION
WITH MUIR OUT OF THE RACE REX WAS INSURED VICTORY.
Special to The Journal
by Allen Gator
The sex scandal and the following suicide of Kirkpatrick Muir ended what seemed to be a sure win for the candidate. Though his pro-environment and neo-Luddite
he had none of Rex's understanding of our
RACIAL TENSIONS MOUNT OVER HOWARD STREET MURDER TRIAL
NEWS
REX RULES
BUTT
SPUN
THE JOURNAL
REX WINS LANDSLIDE REELECTION
MISSING
BETTY RUSSELL
REWARD
PLEASE HELP
BANK
PLEASE ENTER YOUR PIN NUMBER
BALANCE $0.00 ACCOUNT CLOSED.

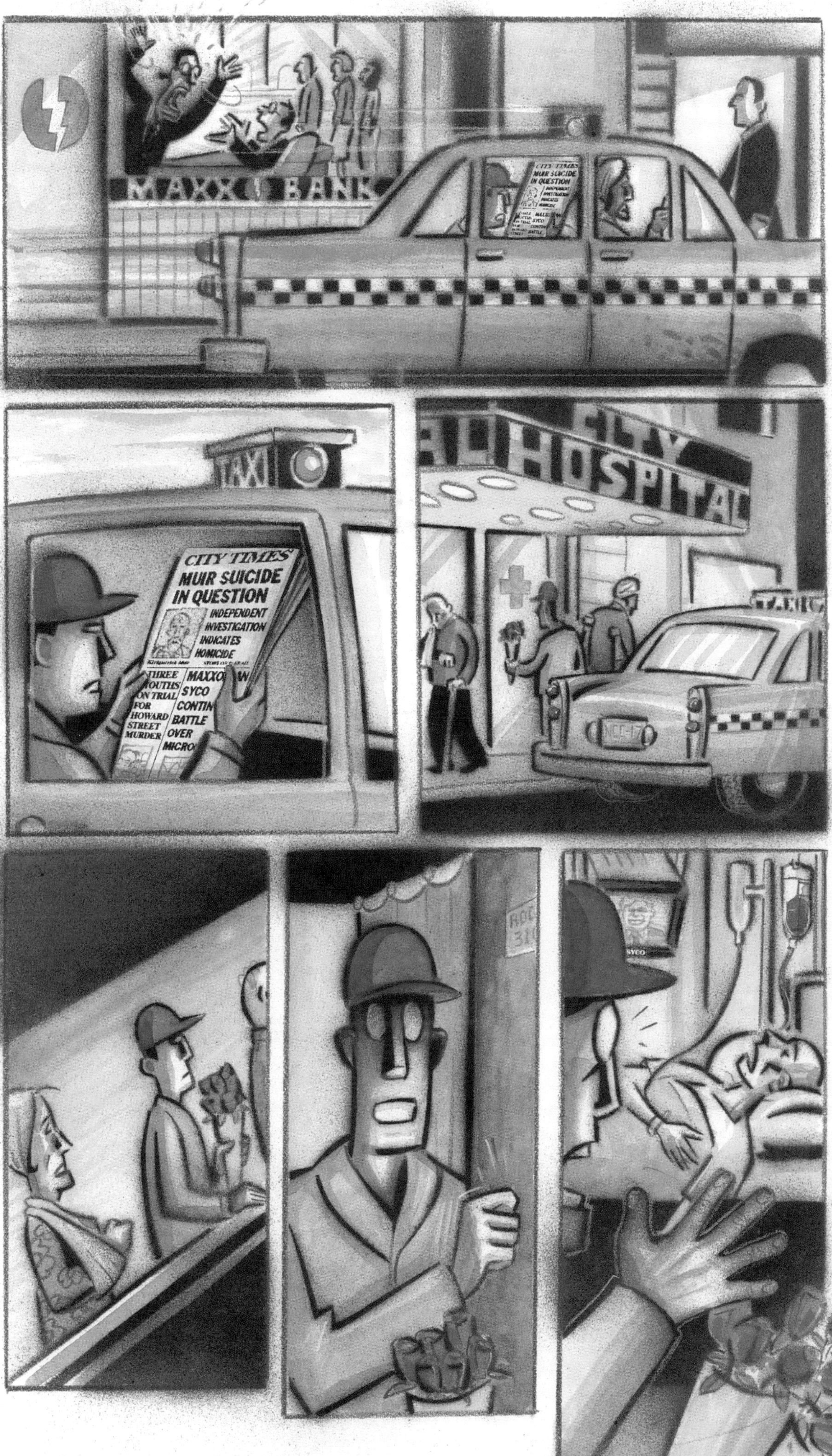
MAXX BANK
CITY TIMES
MUIR SUICIDE IN QUESTION
INDEPENDENT INVESTIGATION INDICATES HOMICIDE
THREE YOUTHS ON TRIAL FOR HOWARD STREET MURDER
SYCO
BATTLE
OVER
TAXI
HOSPITAL
SYCO

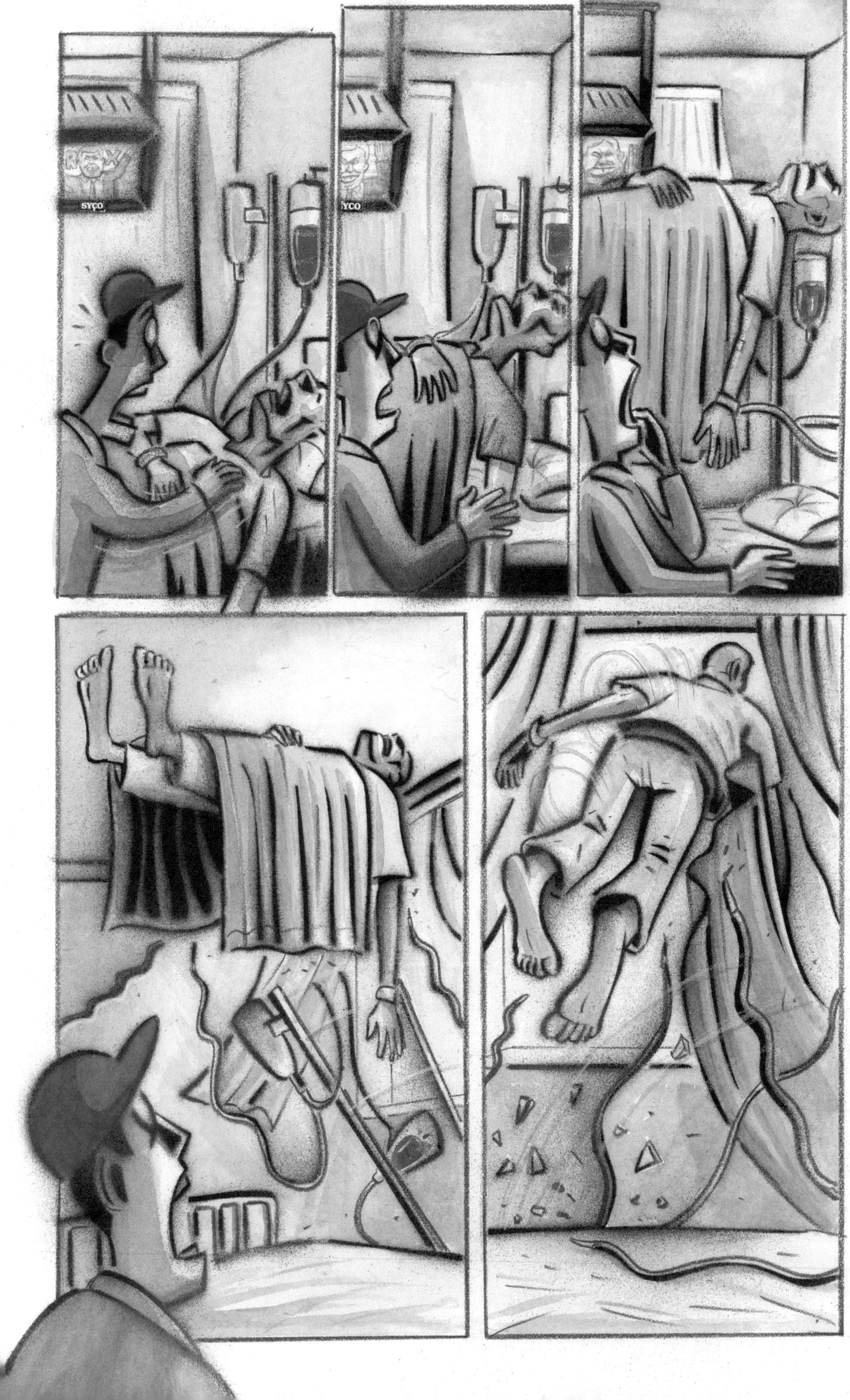
SYÇO

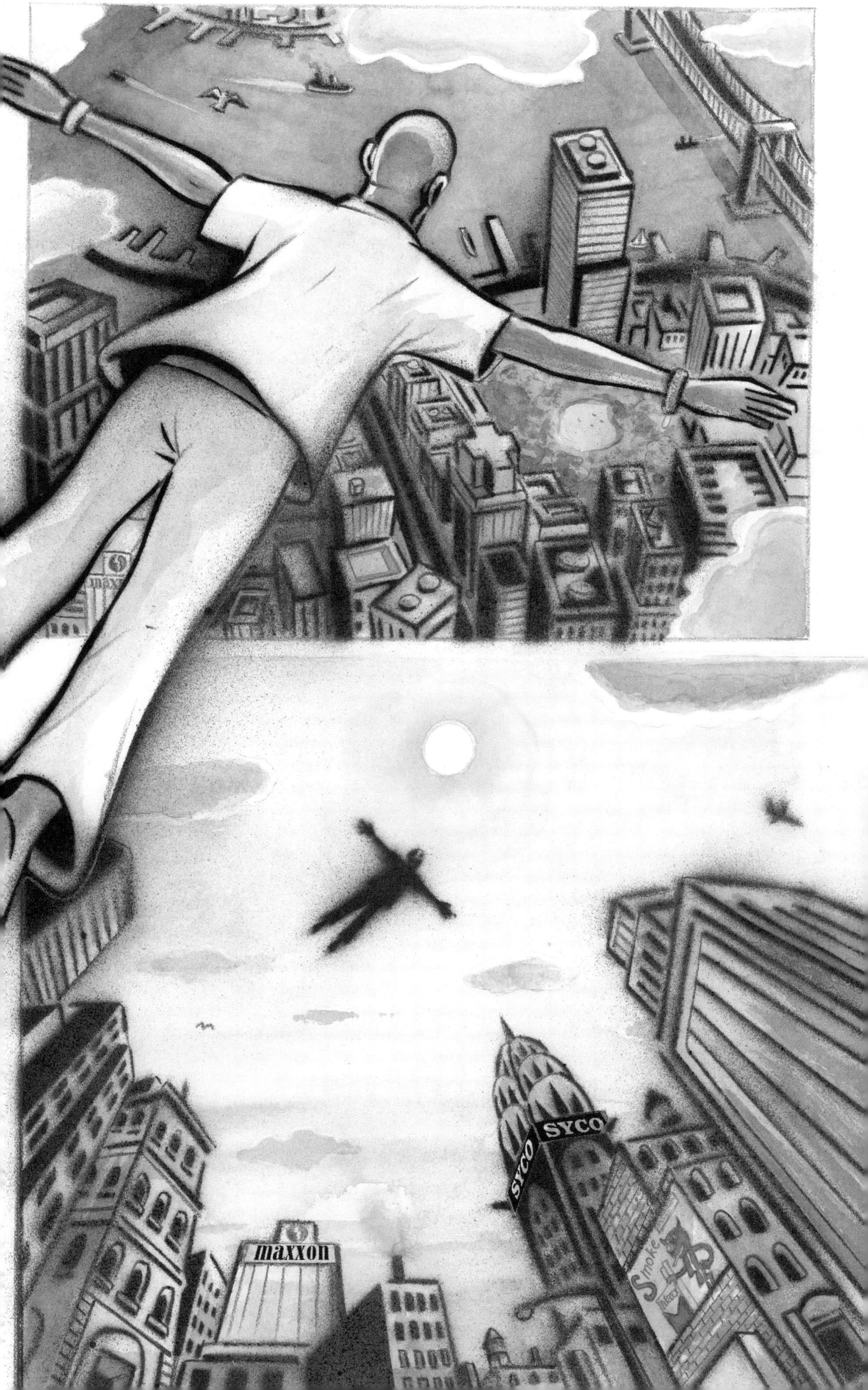
maxxon
SYCO
SYCO
Smoke

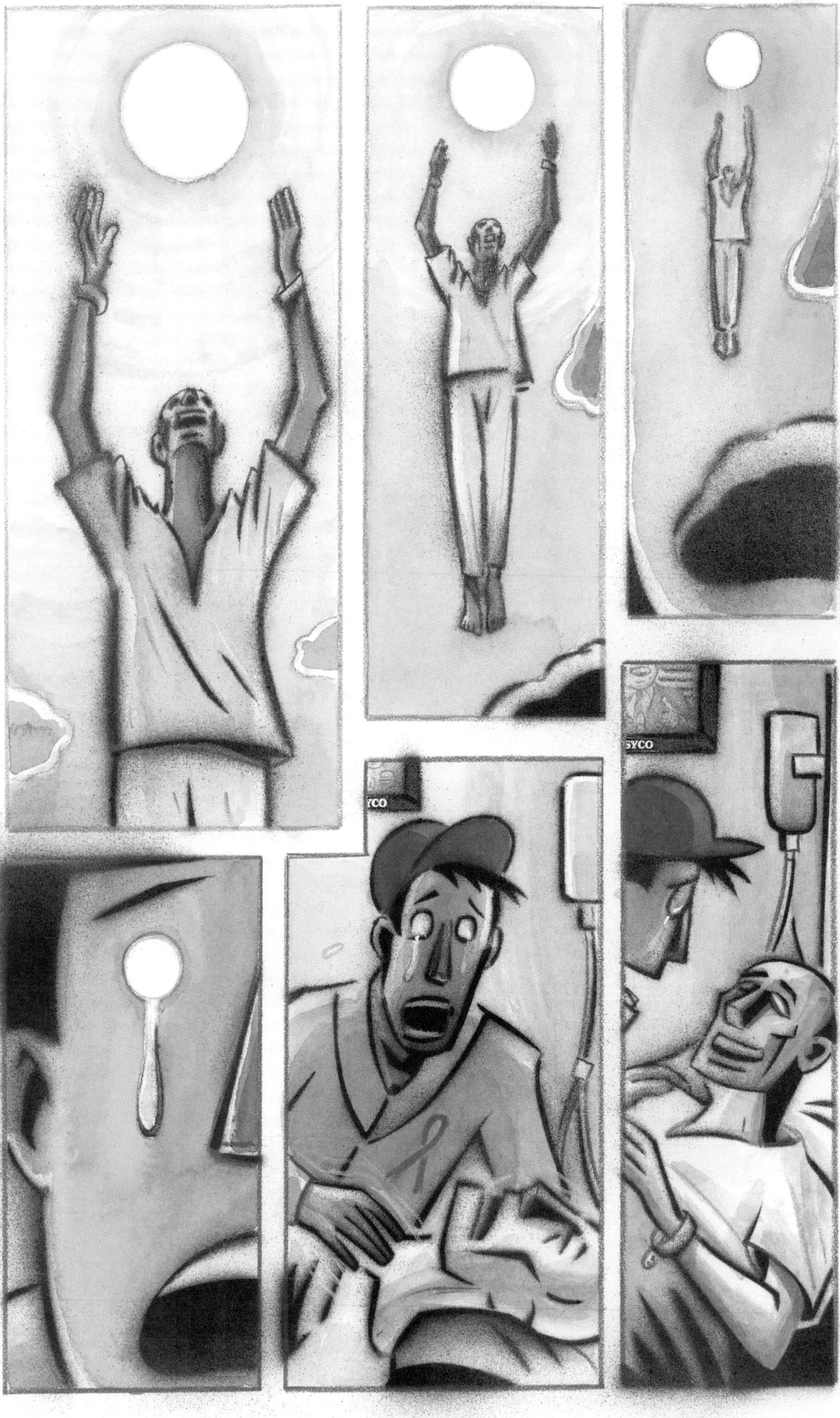
SYCO
SYCO

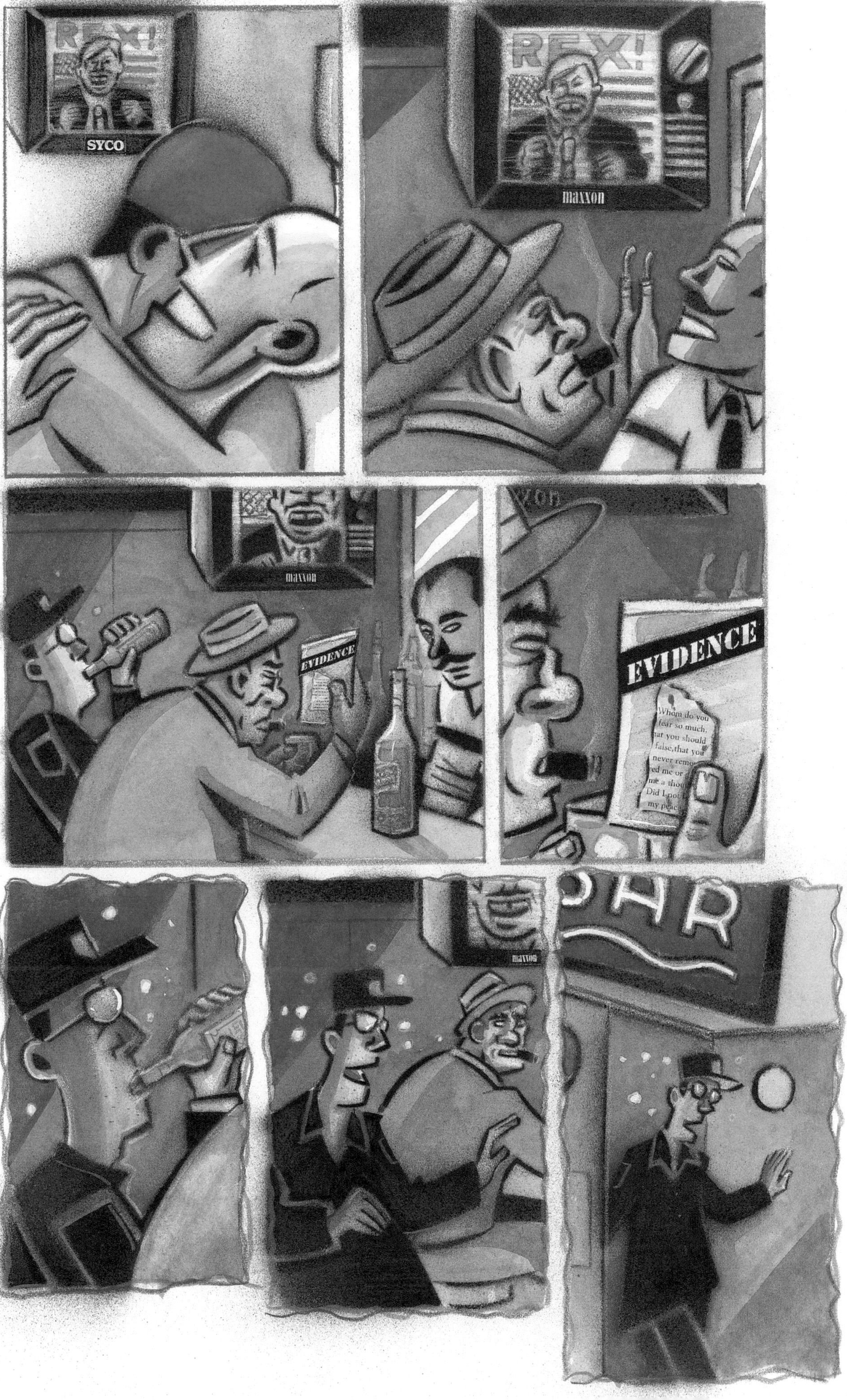
REX!
SYCO
REX!
maxxon
maxxon
EVIDENCE
EVIDENCE
Whom do you
fear so much,
hat you should
false,that you
never remo
red me or
me a thou
Did I not
my peac
maxxon

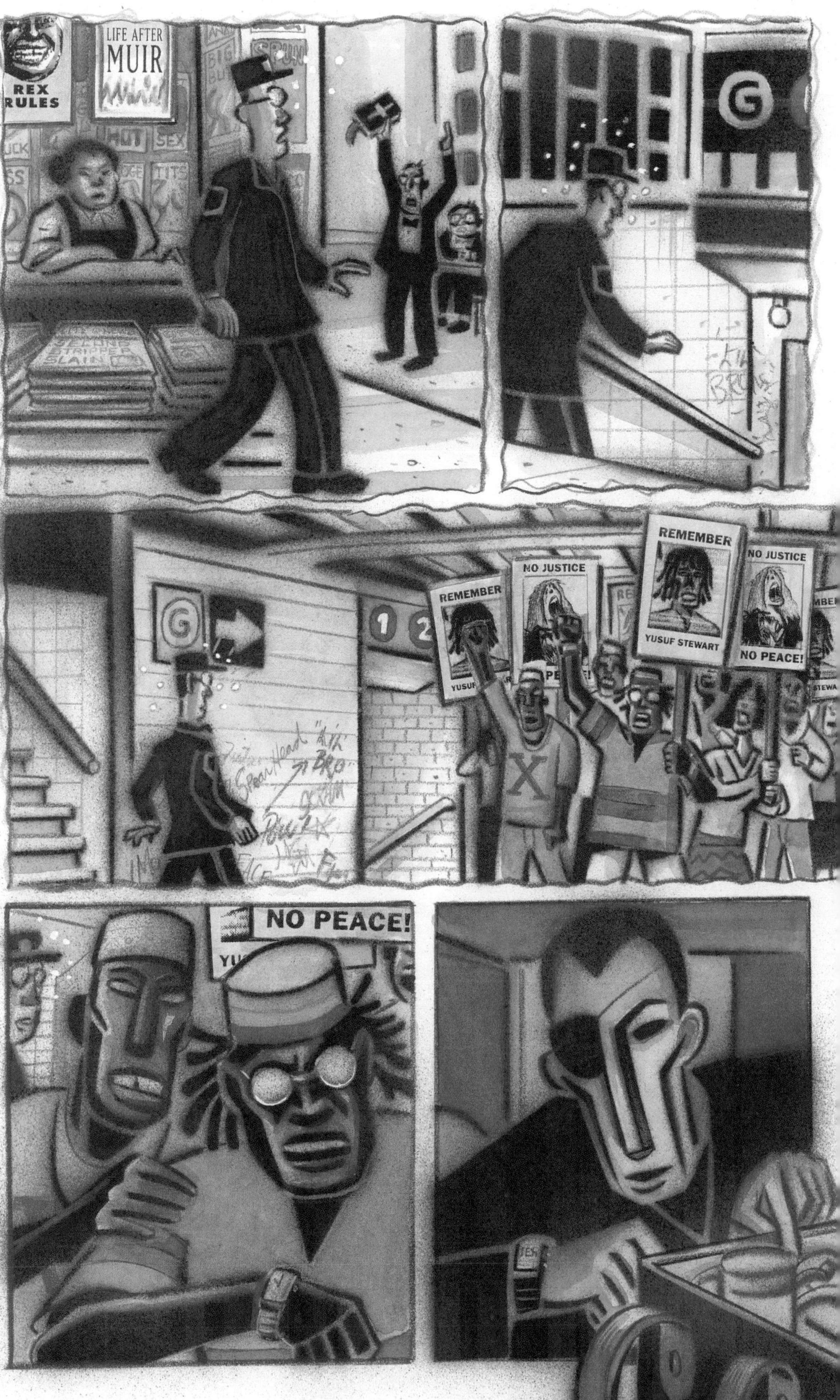
REX RULES
LIFE AFTER MUIR
HOT
SEX
TITS
STRIPPER SLAIN
G
G
1 2
REMEMBER
NO JUSTICE
REMEMBER
YUSUF STEWART
NO JUSTICE
NO PEACE!
NO PEACE!

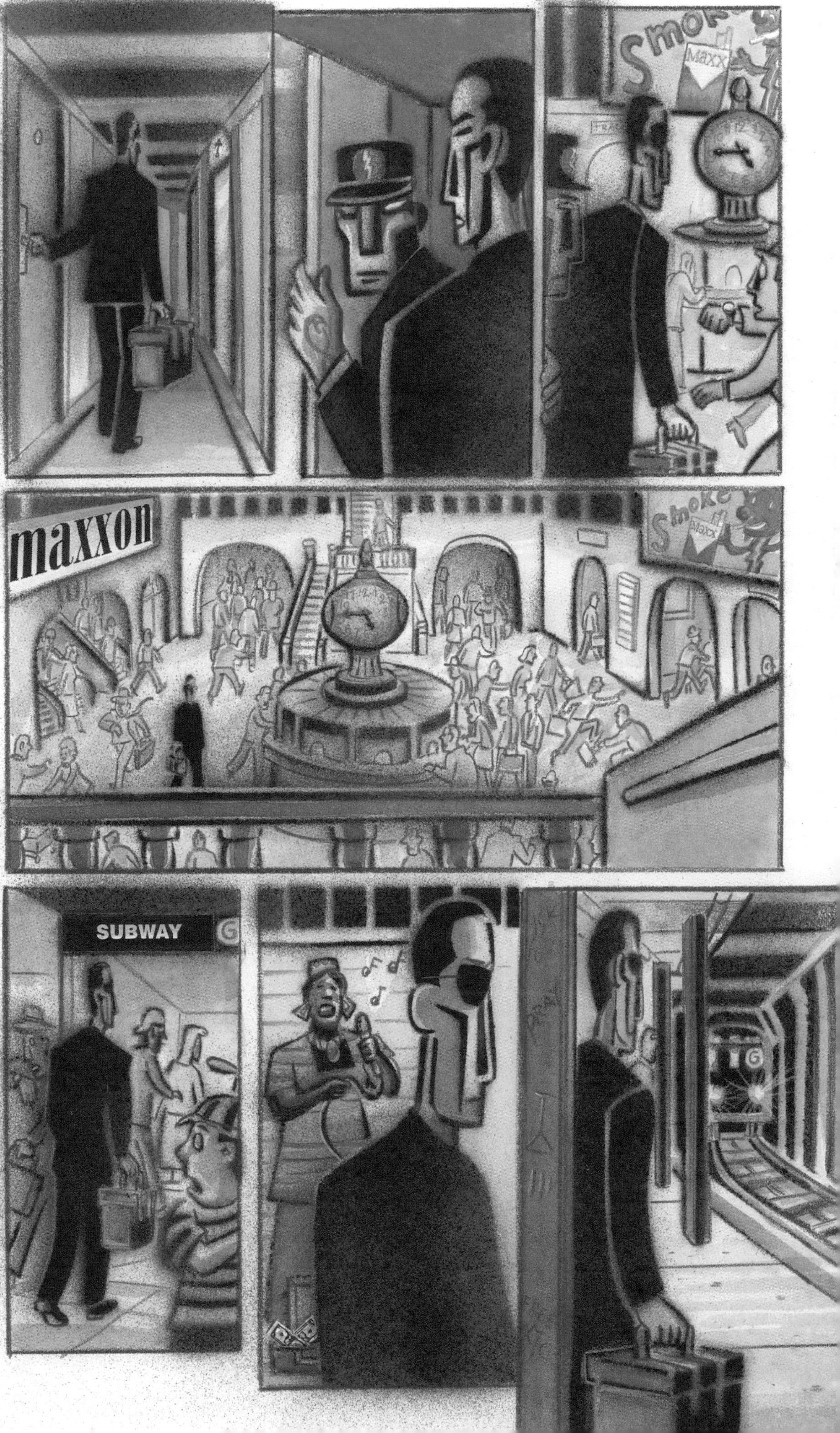
MAXX
maxxon
Smoke
Maxx
SUBWAY
G

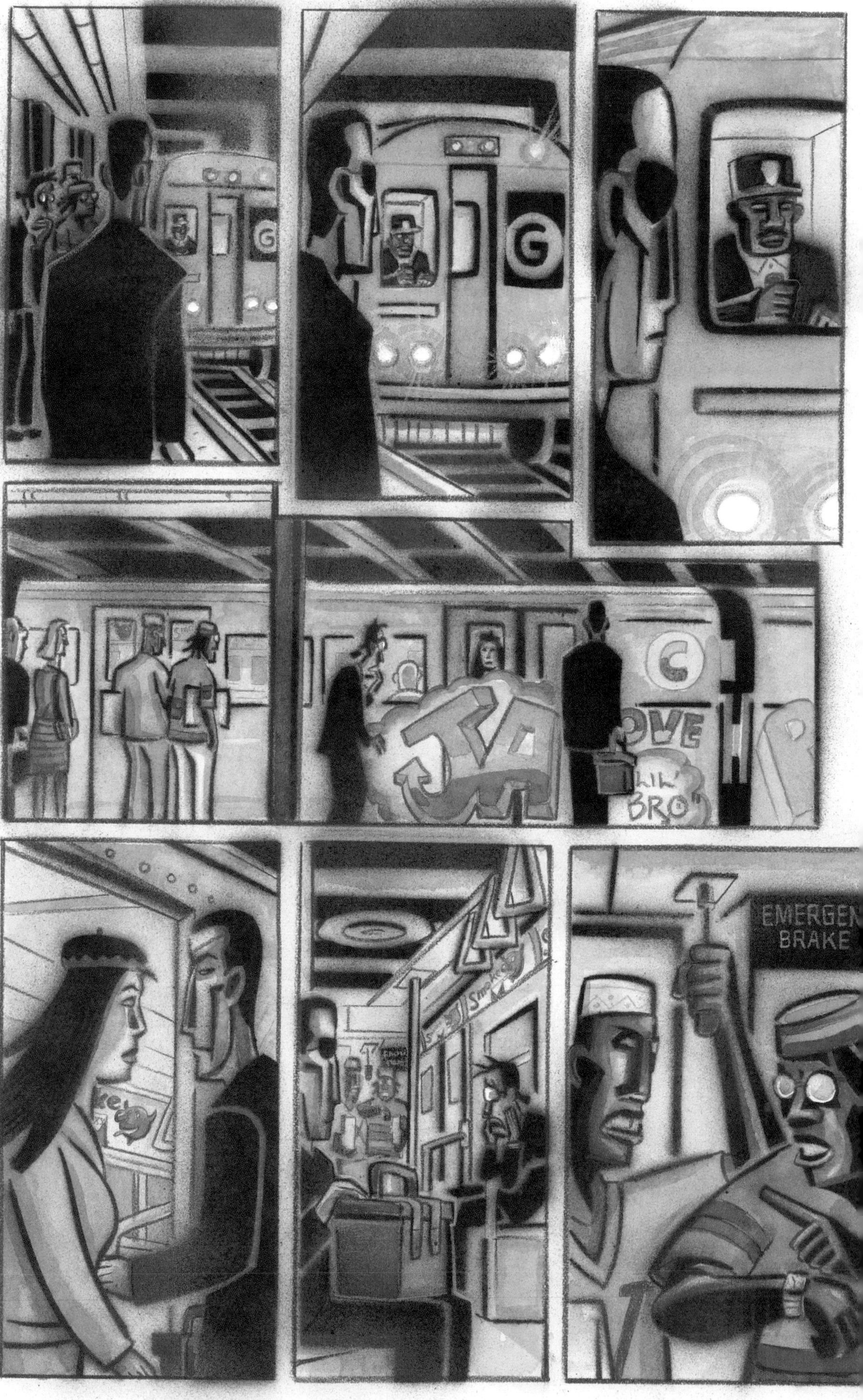
G
G
EMERGEN
BRAKE

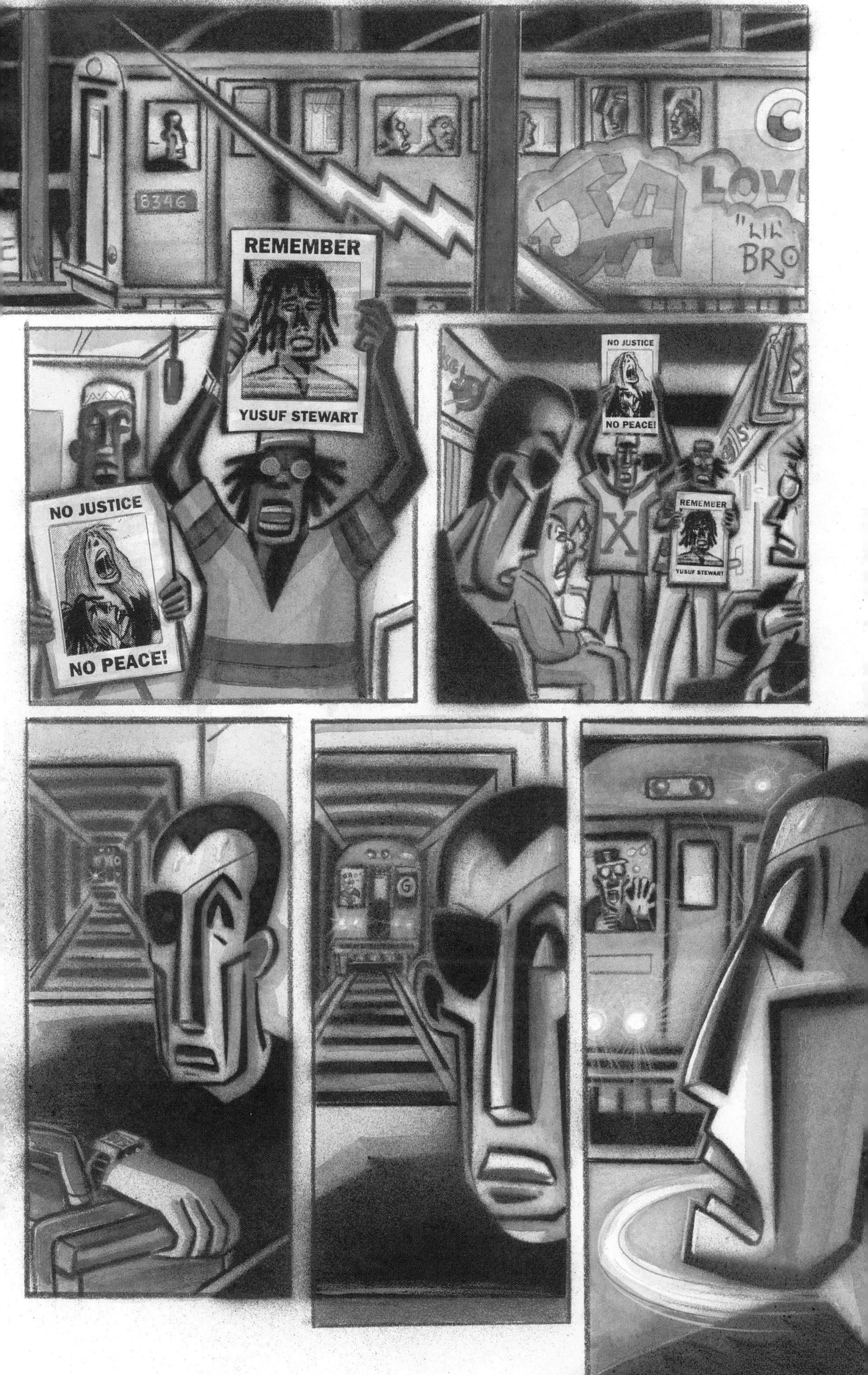
8346
REMEMBER
YUSUF STEWART
NO JUSTICE
NO PEACE!
NO JUSTICE
NO PEACE!
REMEMBER
YUSUF STEWART
G

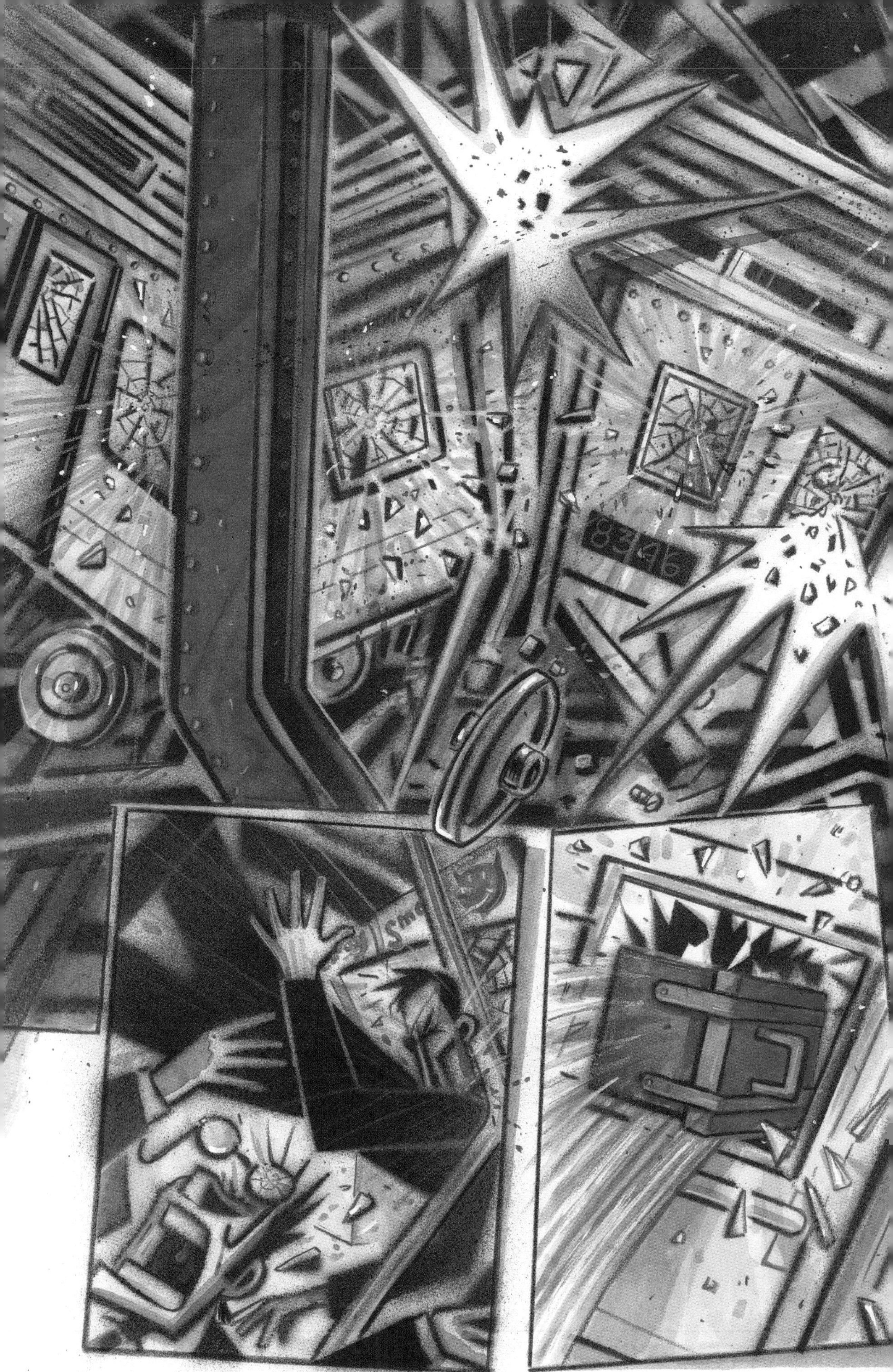
8346

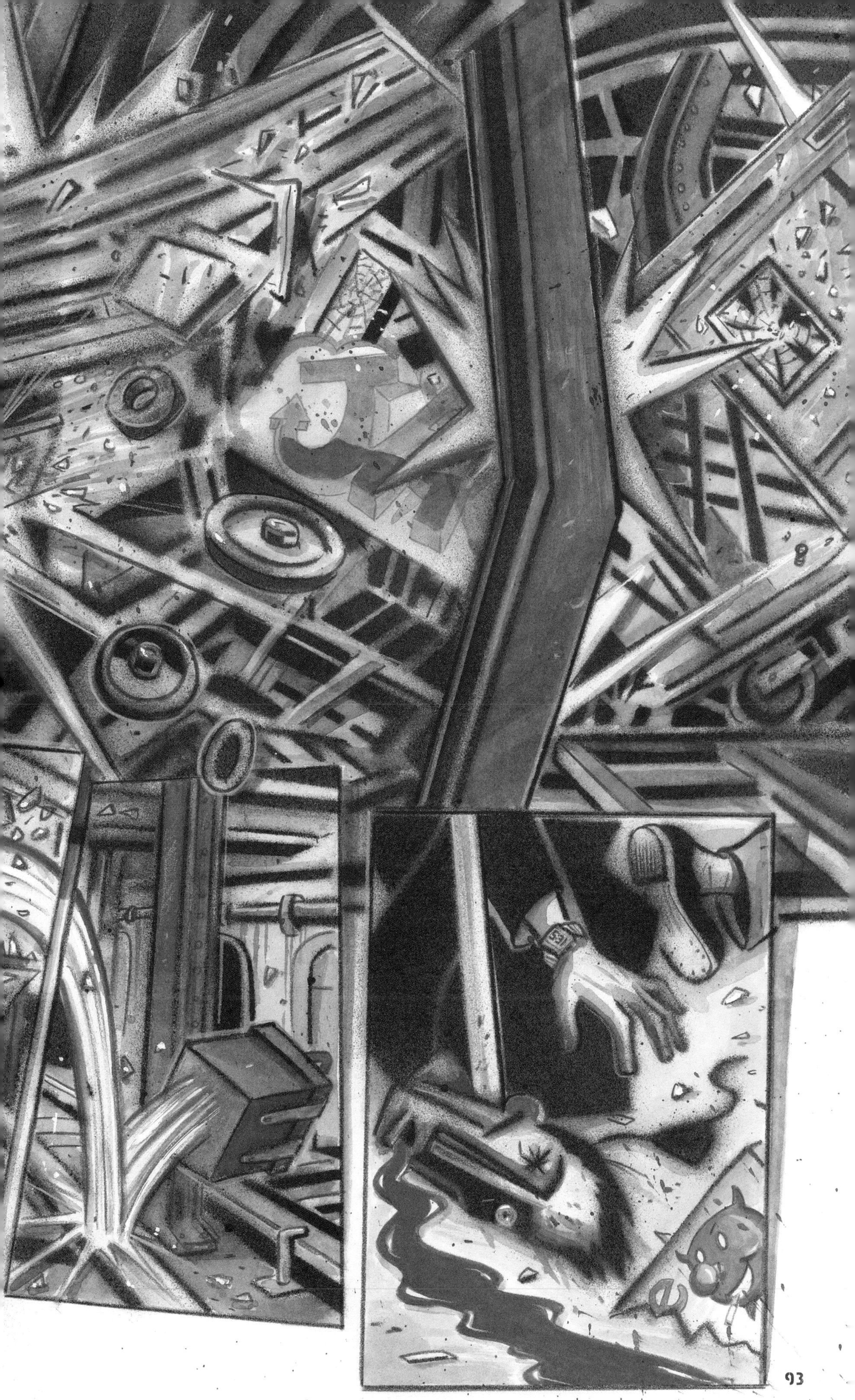

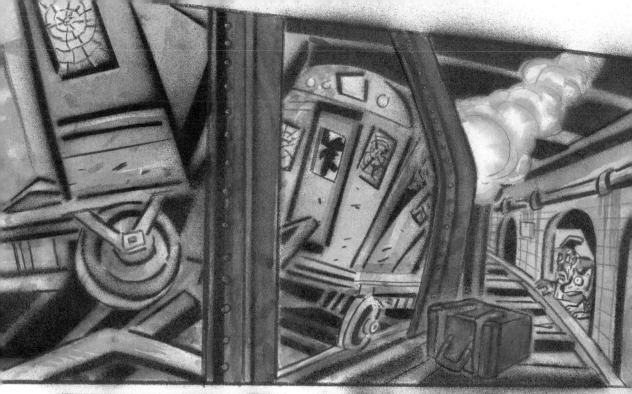

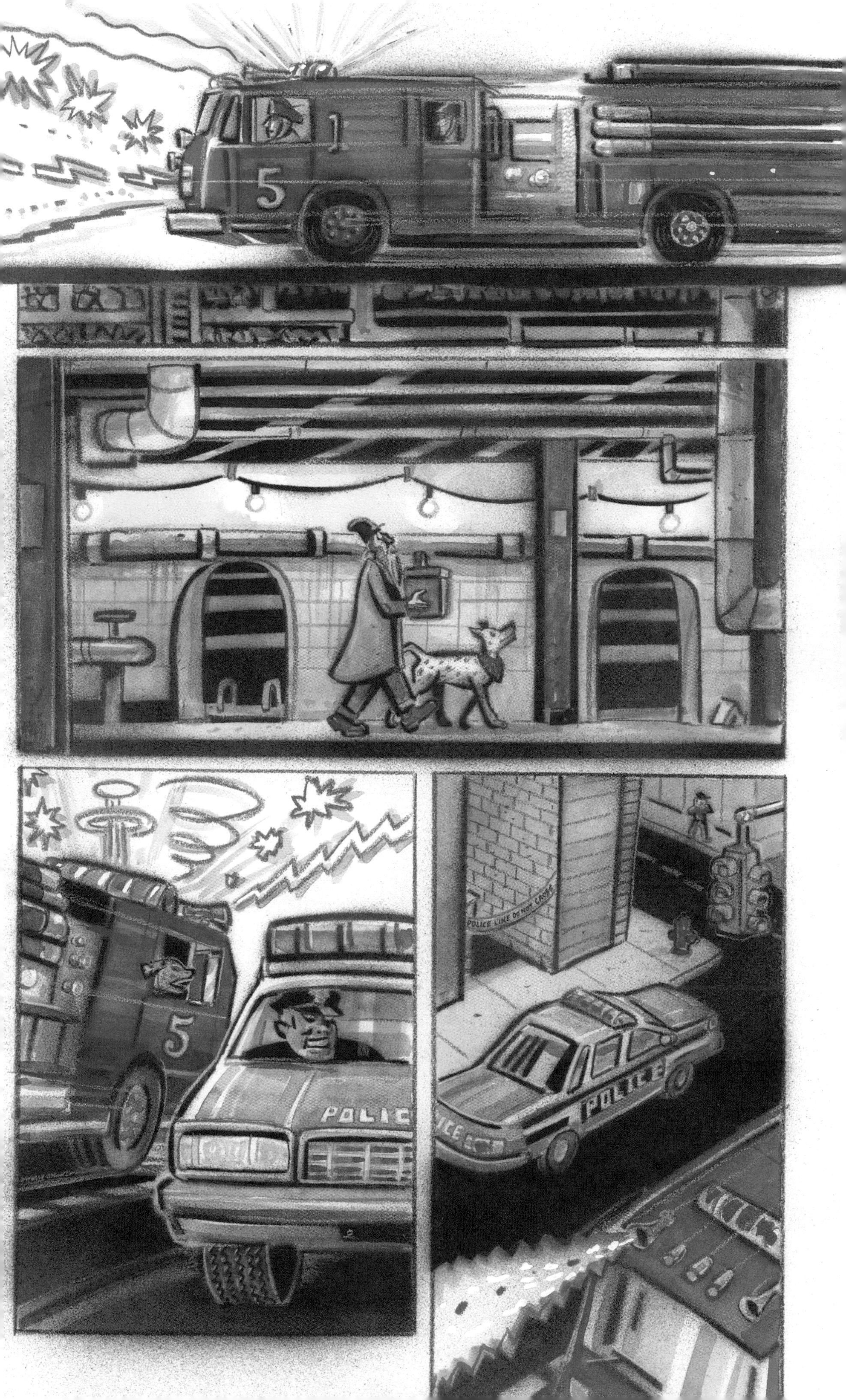
5
5
POLIC
POLICE LINE DO NOT CROSS
POLICE

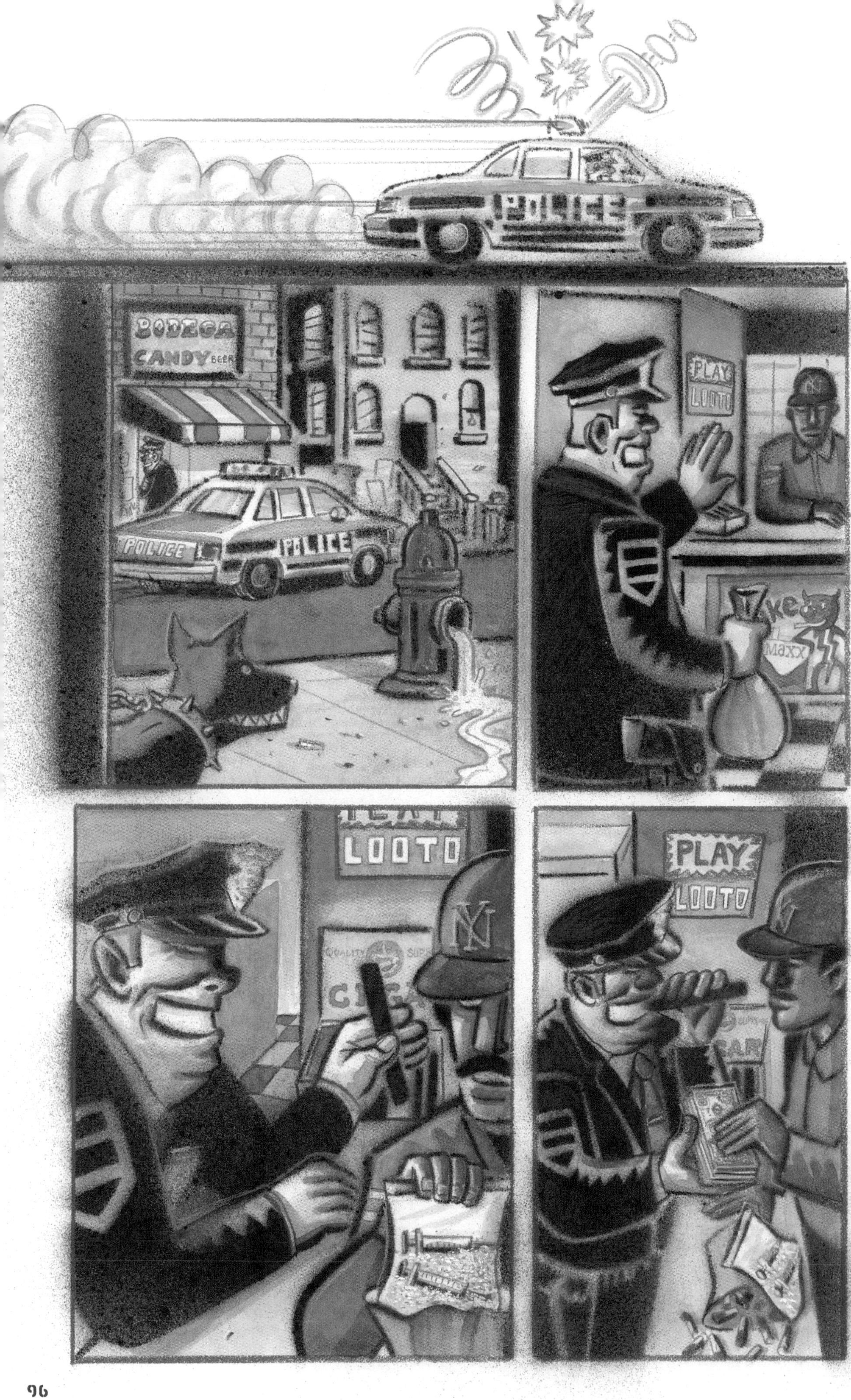
POLICE
BODEGA
CANDY BEER
POLICE
POLICE
PLAY
LOOTO
MAXX
LOOTO
PLAY
LOOTO

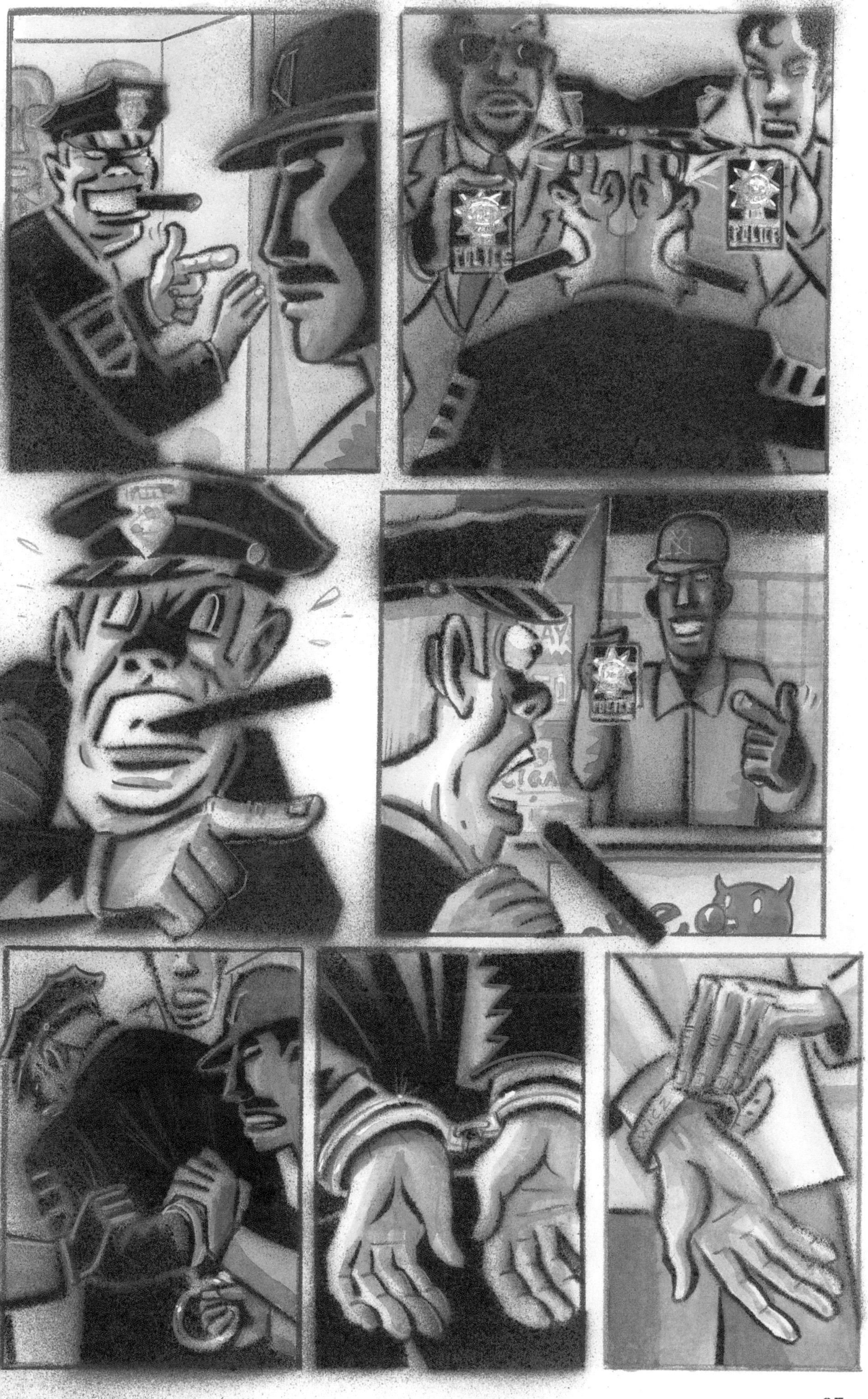

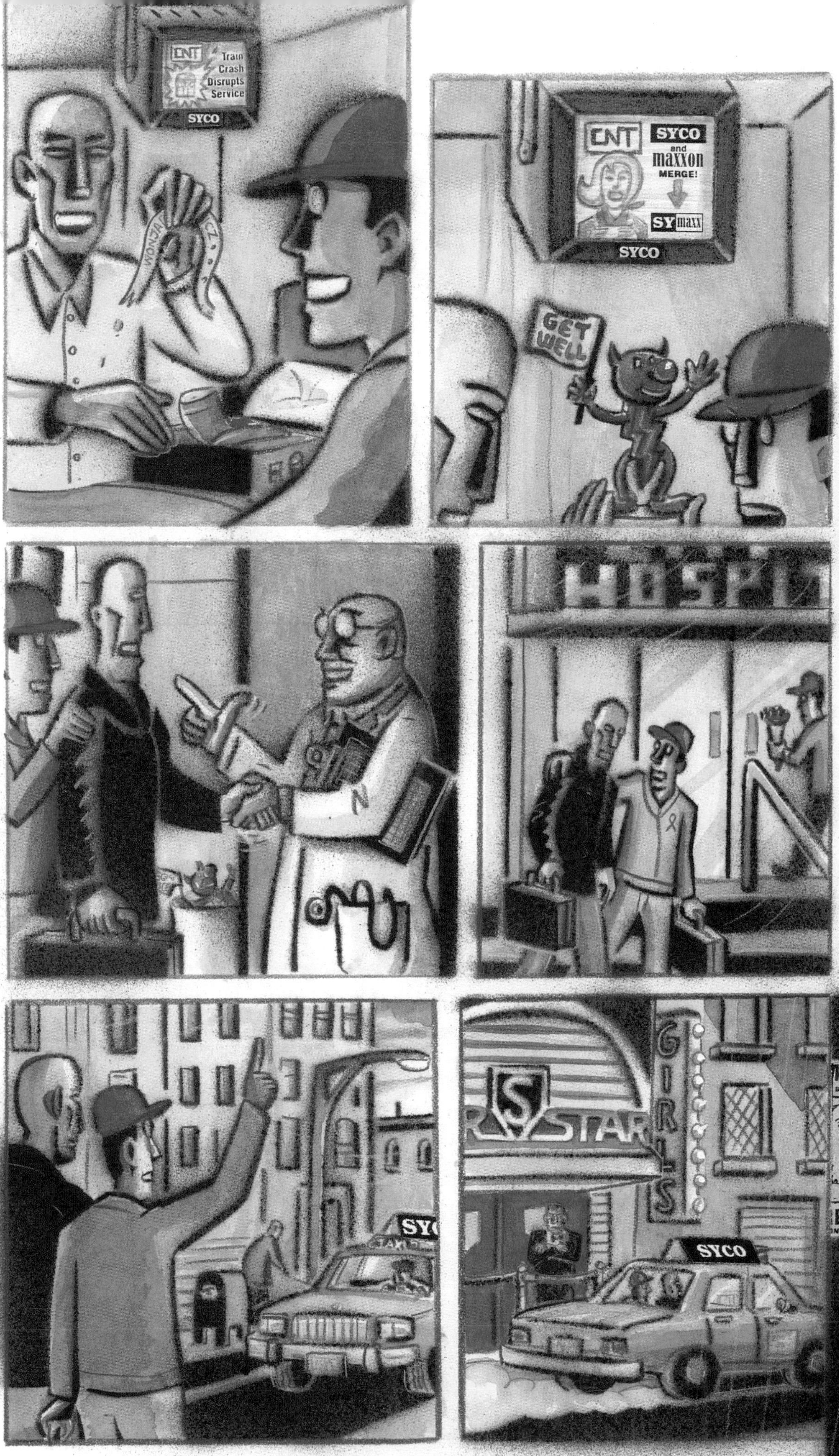
CNT
Train Crash Disrupts Service
SYCO
CNT
SYCO and maxxon MERGE!
SYmaxx
SYCO
GET WELL
SYCO
STAR
GIRLS
SYCO

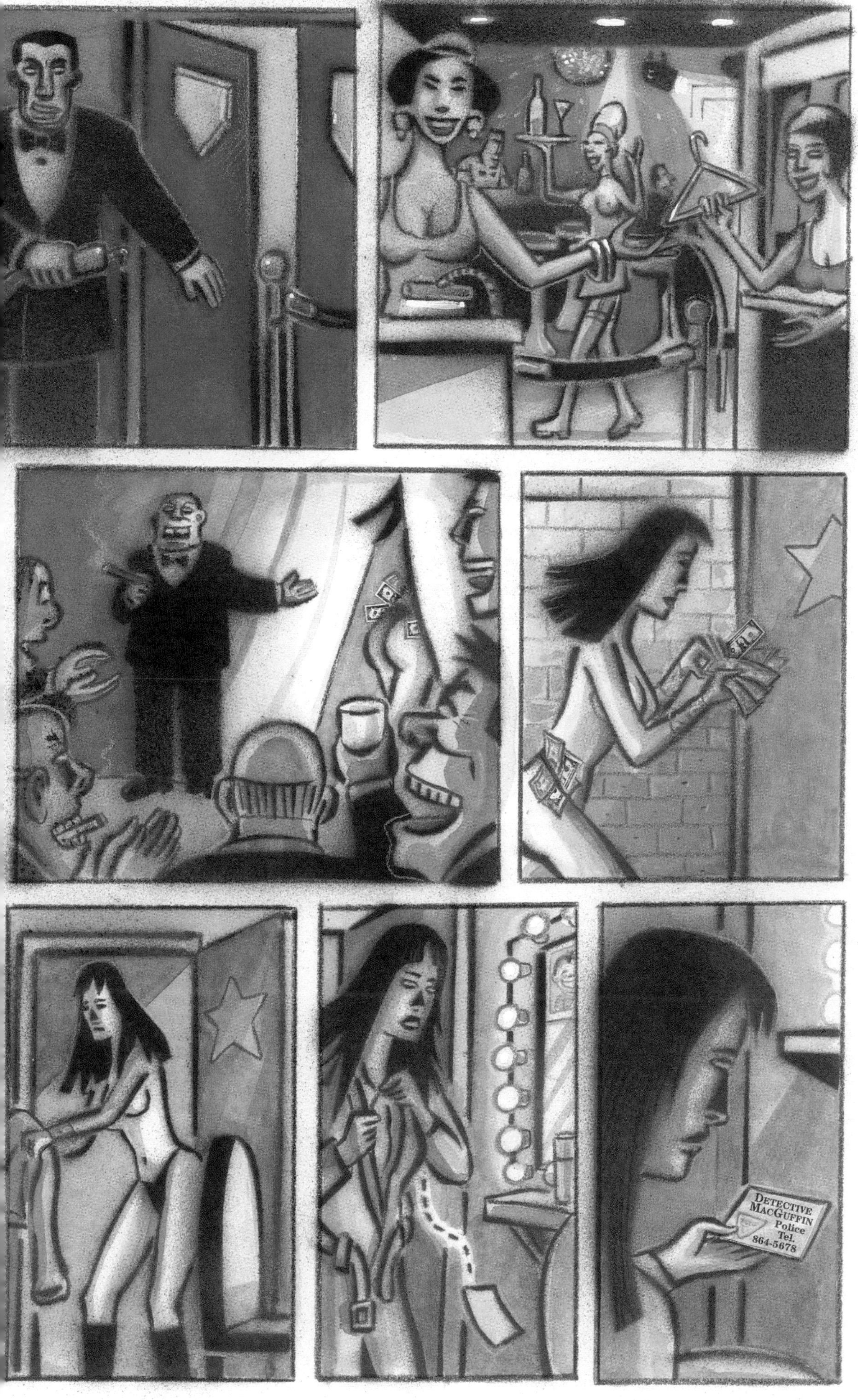
DETECTIVE
MacGUFFIN
Police
Tel.
864-5678

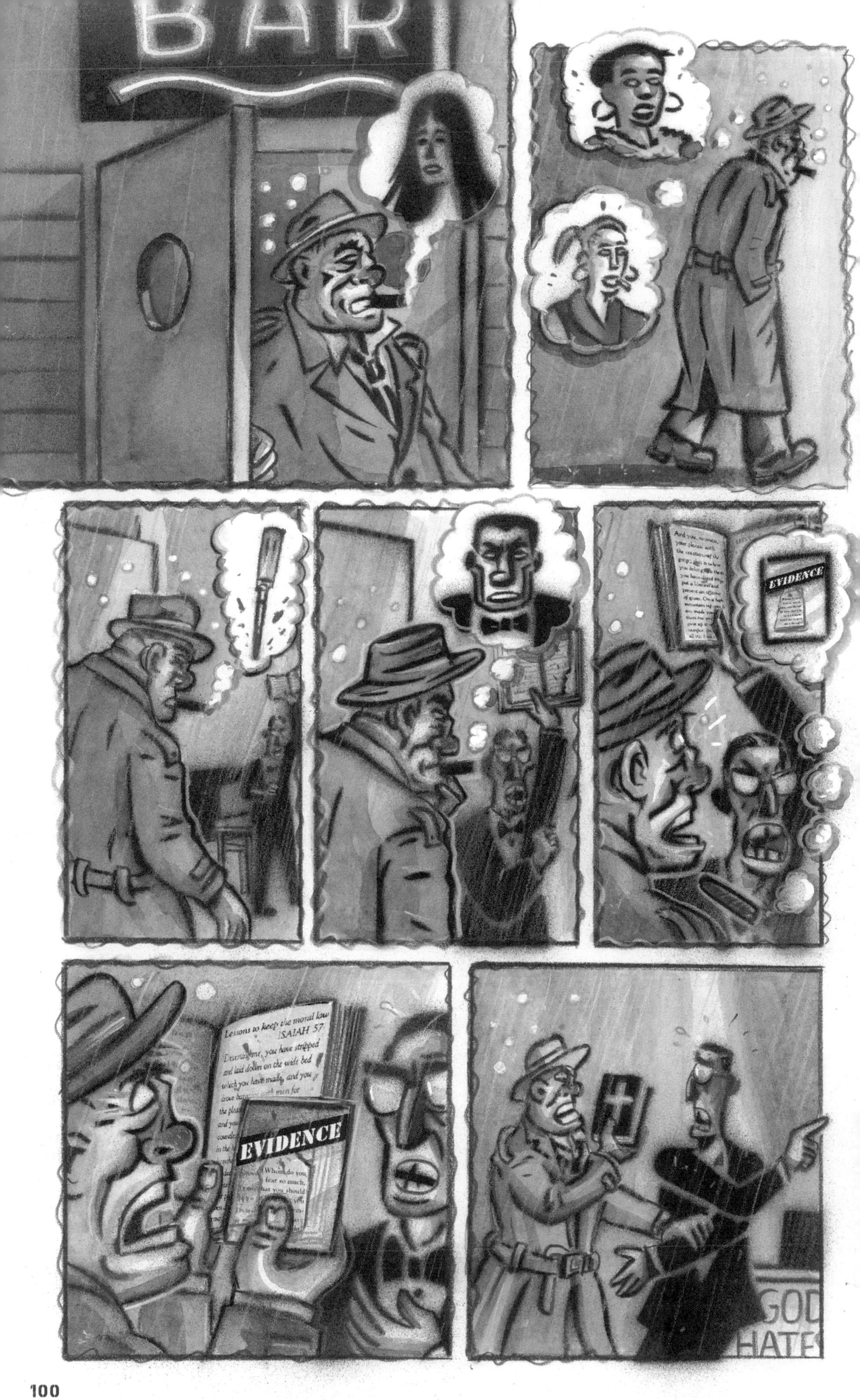

BAR
EVIDENCE
Lessons to keep the moral law
ISAIAH 57
you have stripped
and laid down on the wide bed
which you have made, and you
EVIDENCE
Whom do you
fear so much,
GOD

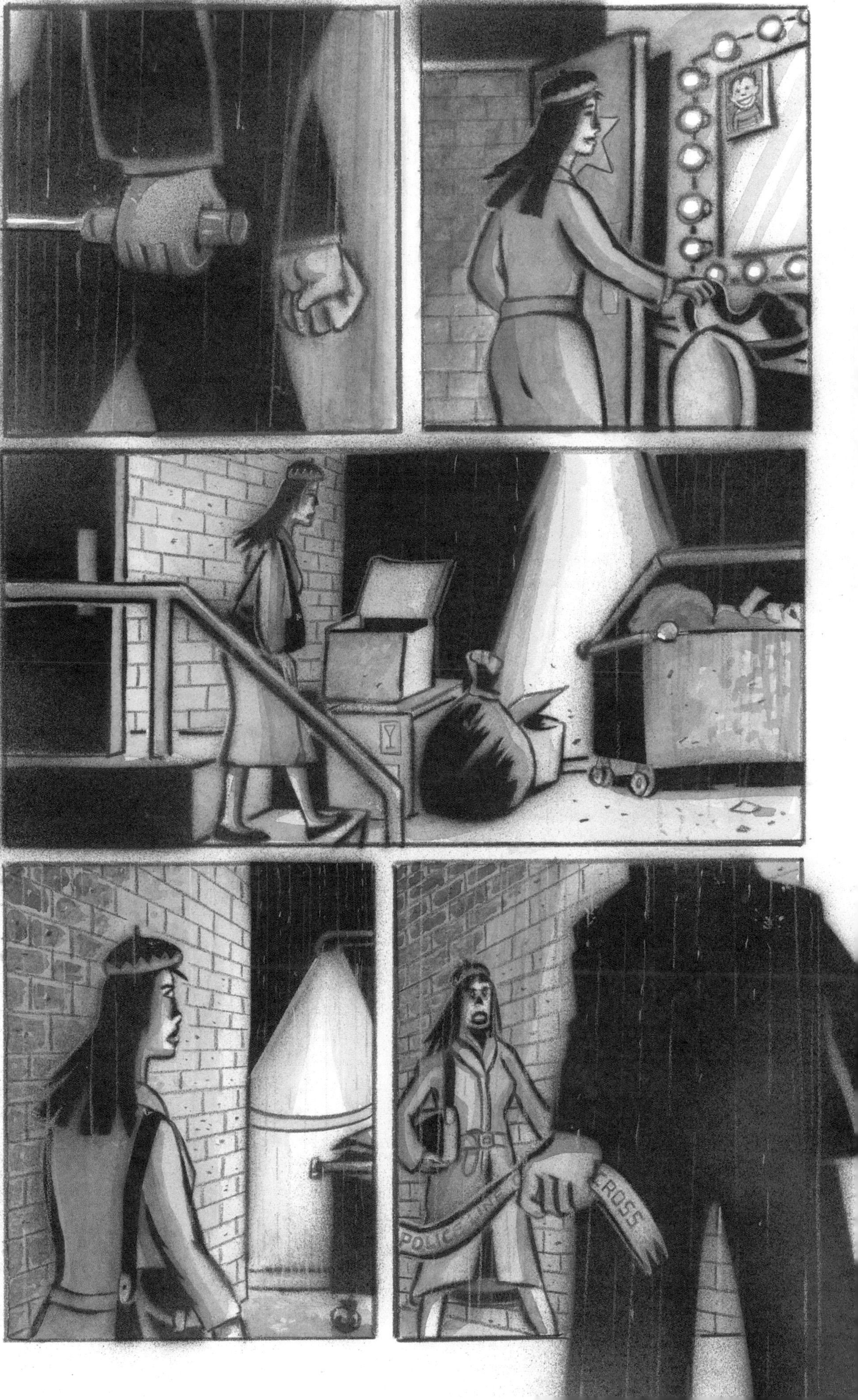
POLIC
CROSS

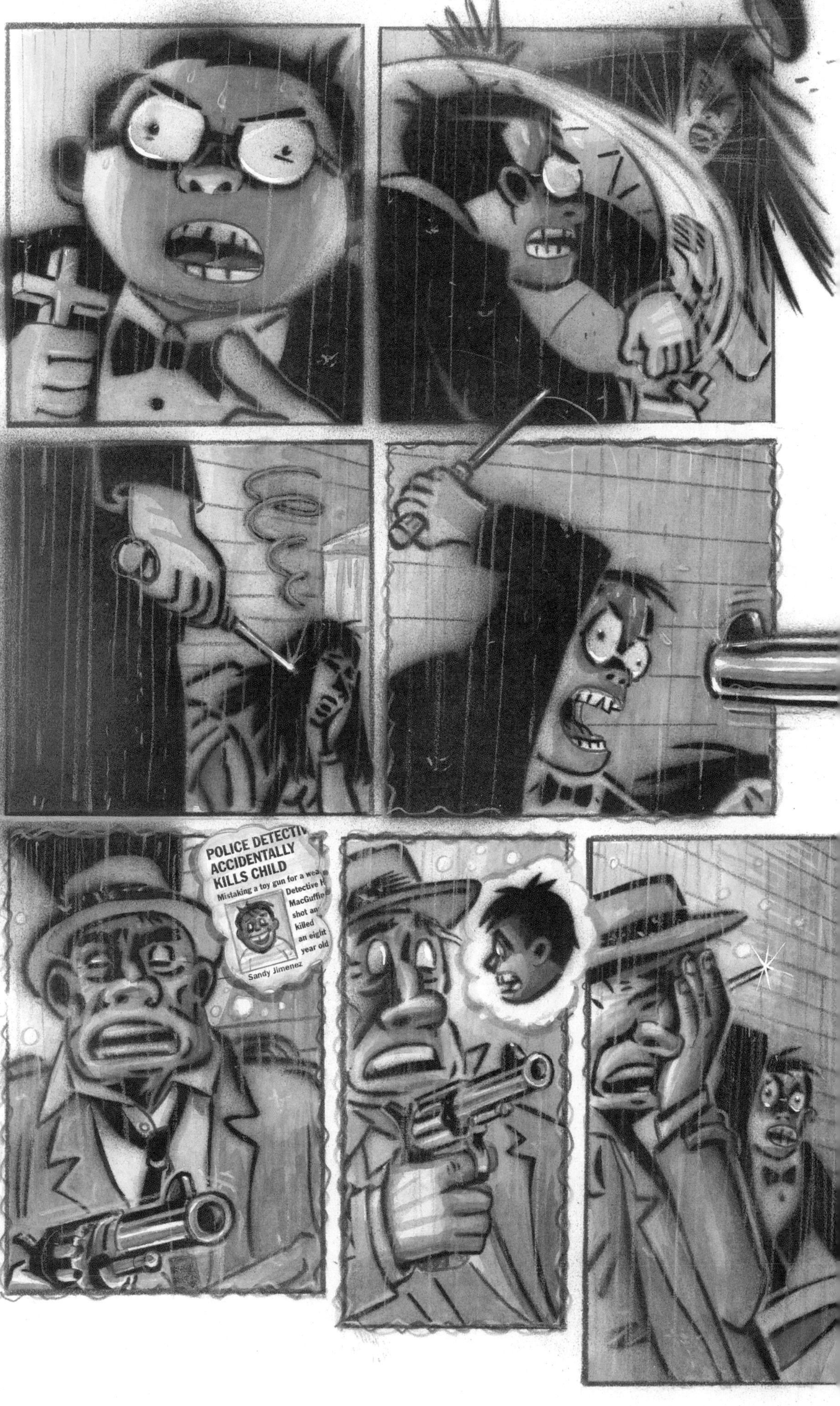
POLICE DETECTIV
ACCIDENTALLY
KILLS CHILD
Mistaking a toy gun for a wea
Detective H
MacGuffin
shot an
killed
an eight
year old
Sandy Jimenez

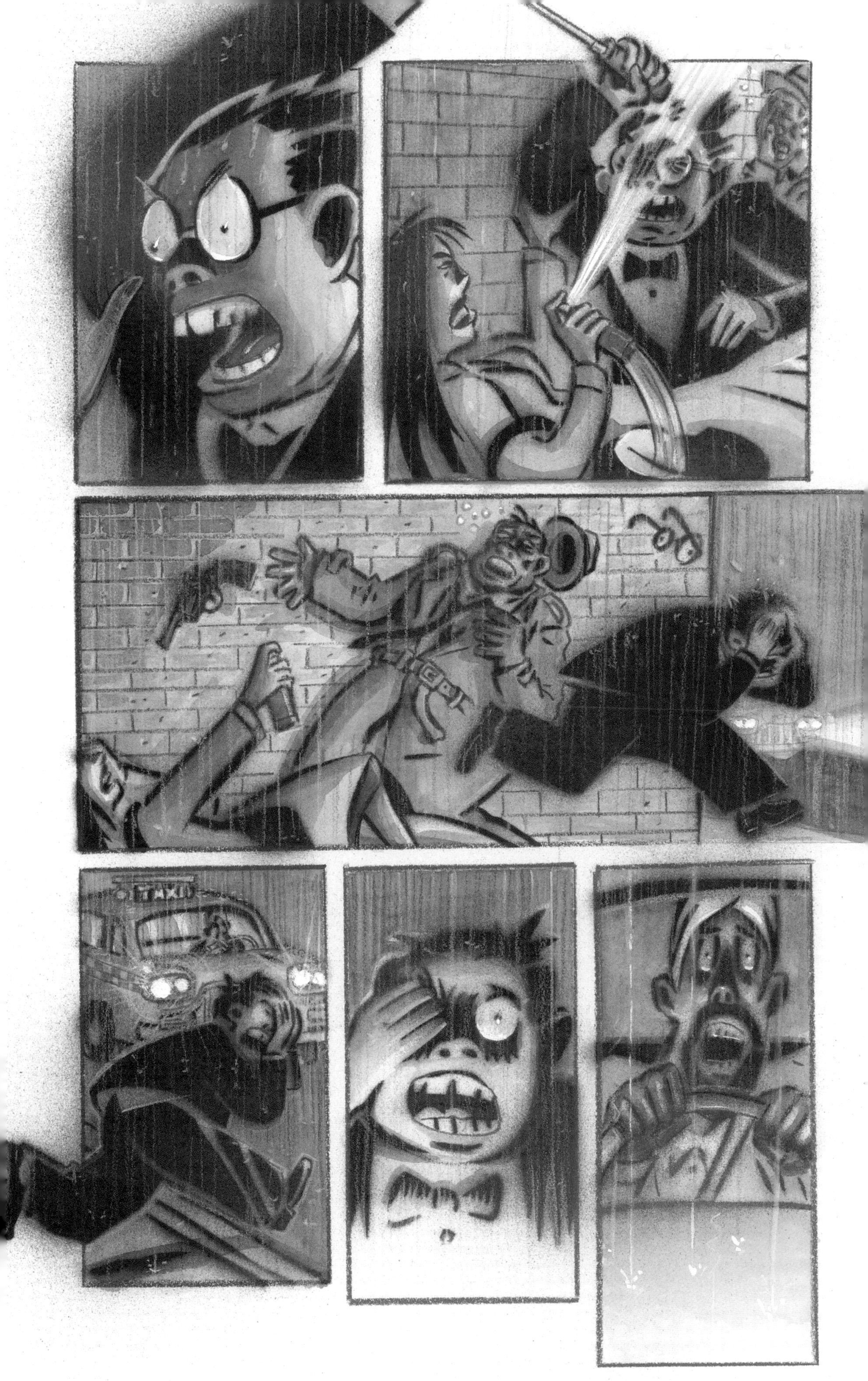
TAXI

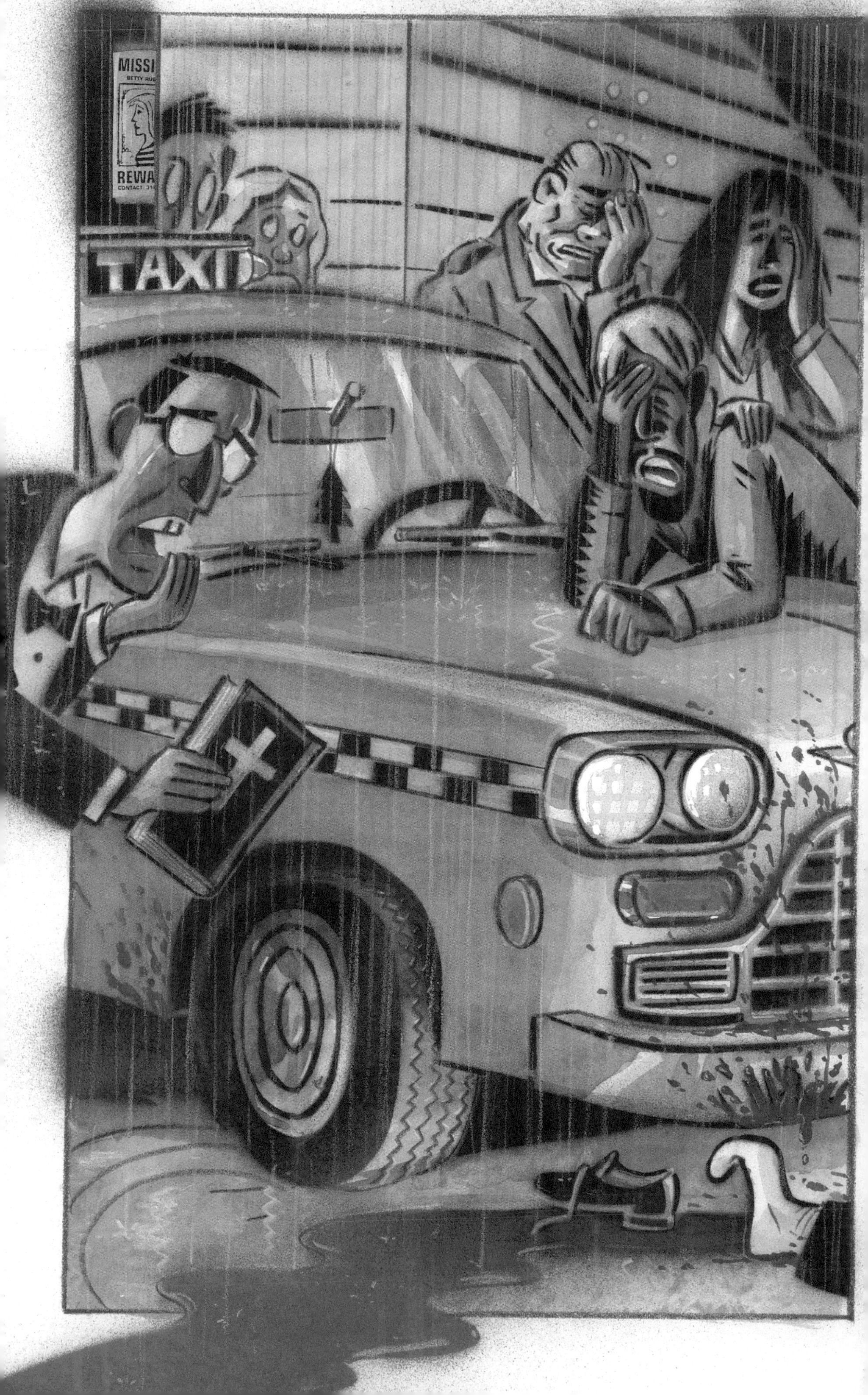
MISSI
REWA
TAXI

EPILOGUE

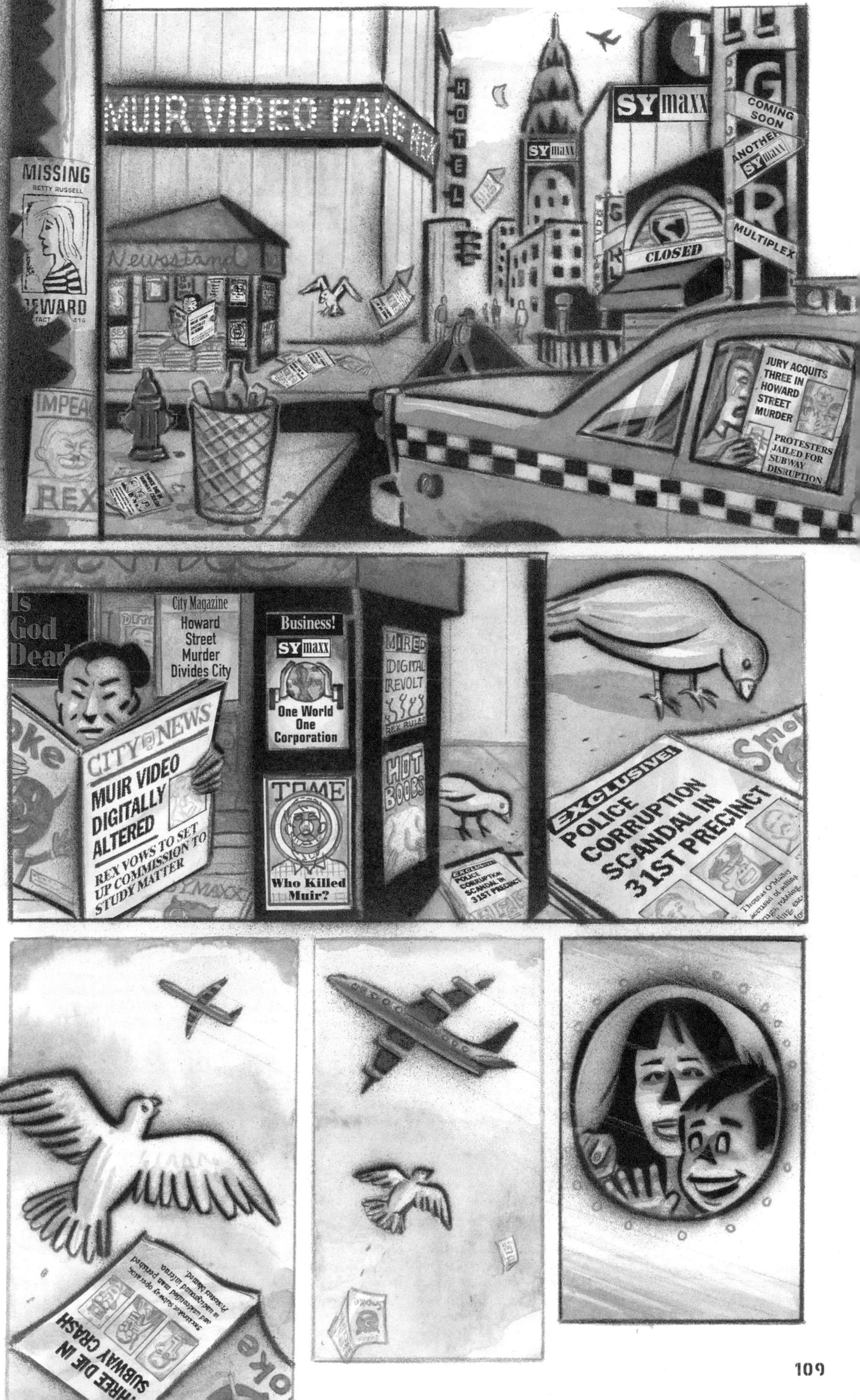
MUIR VIDEO FAKE REX
MISSING
BETTY RUSSELL
HOTEL
SYmaxx
SYmaxx
COMING SOON
ANOTHER SYmaxx
MULTIPLEX
CLOSED
Newsstand
REX
JURY ACQUITS THREE IN HOWARD STREET MURDER
PROTESTERS JAILED FOR SUBWAY DISRUPTION
Is God Dead
City Magazine
Howard Street Murder Divides City
CITY NEWS
MUIR VIDEO DIGITALLY ALTERED
REX VOWS TO SET UP COMMISSION TO STUDY MATTER
Business!
SYmaxx
One World One Corporation
MIRED DIGITAL REVOLT
REX RULES
HOT BOOBS
TIME
Who Killed Muir?
EXCLUSIVE!
POLICE CORRUPTION SCANDAL IN 31ST PRECINCT
THREE DIE IN SUBWAY CRASH

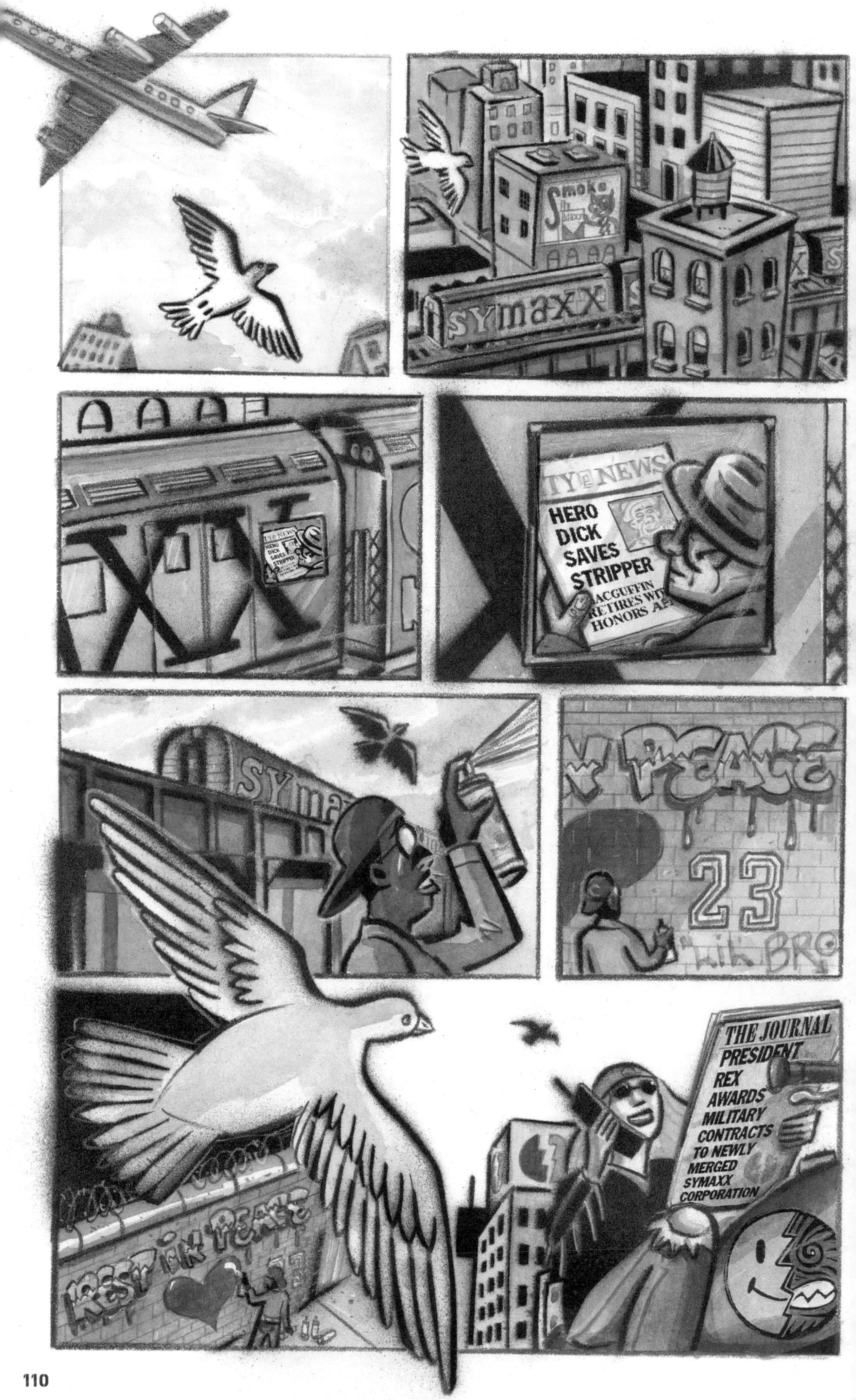
SYMAXX
HERO DICK SAVES STRIPPER
PEACE
23
THE JOURNAL
PRESIDENT REX AWARDS MILITARY CONTRACTS TO NEWLY MERGED SYMAXX CORPORATION
REST IN PEACE

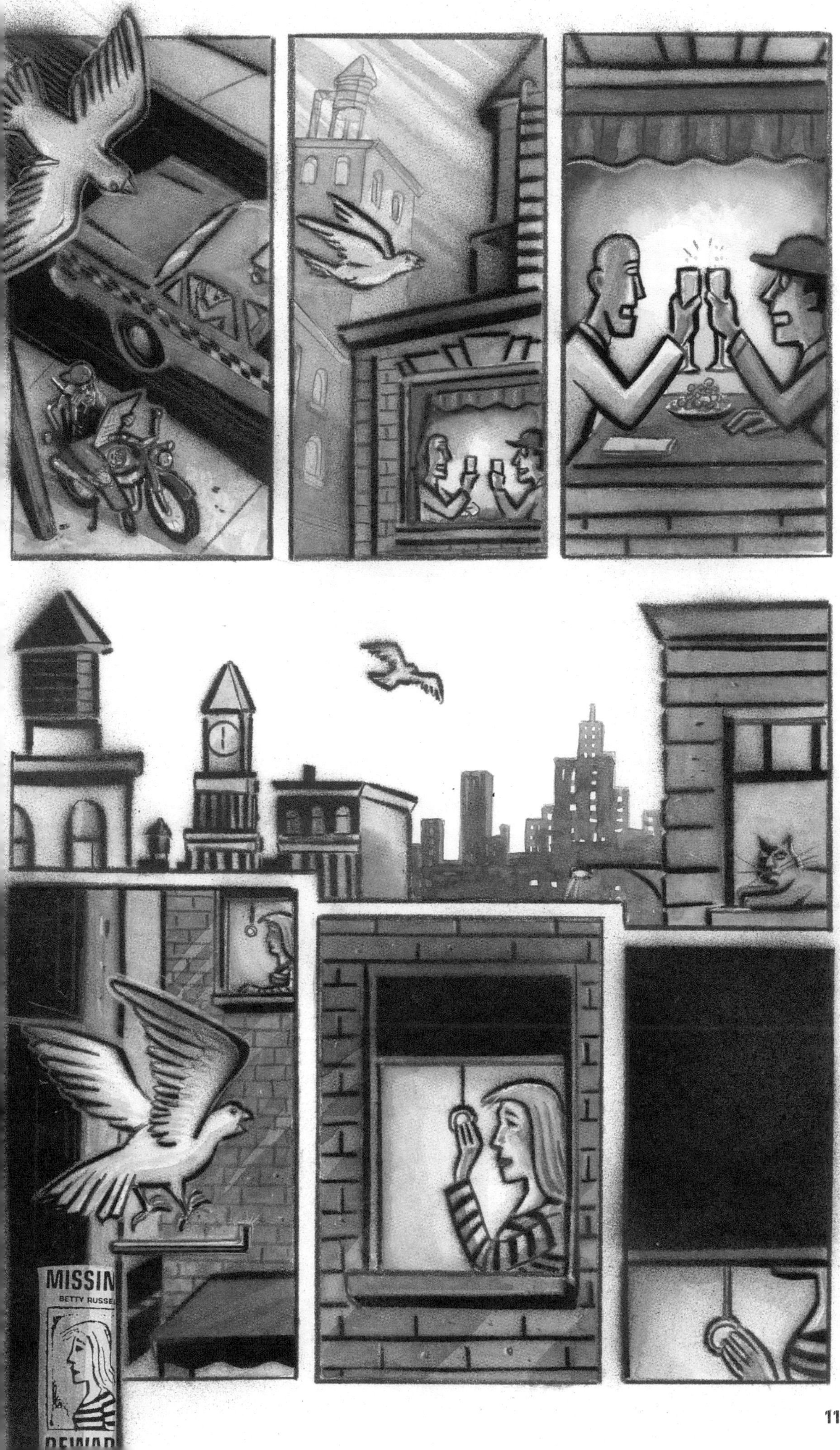
MISSIN
BETTY RUSSE